SILENCE

NELL BRACH, BOOK ONE

S. E. GREEN

PROLOGUE

Gasping, Scarlett tore through the dark woods. The tree limbs reached for her, like long scabby fingers, scraping at her clothes and skin. She slid across a patch of leaves and fallen pine needles, landing behind a cluster of shrubs. Her heart pounded, achingly fast. Her gaze darted through the night. The air around her pulsed with her nerves.

A cool April breeze curled through, and despite the adrenaline spiking in her veins, she shivered. Overhead, the moon glowed full. The pungent, yet sweet scent of the town's brewery clung in the air.

Across the woods, just over there, a welcoming yellow light outlined a home. She was just about to crawl forward when her lungs contracted.

She coughed.

She tried to yell for help, but no words came.

ONE

Monday, 7 a.m.

MY ARMS PUMP, sweat dampens my back, and my long legs devour the six-mile, mulch-covered trail that circles the town's new park.

Up ahead women and men perform downward dog in the sunrise yoga group that meets here every Monday morning, weather permitting.

Wearing a green hoodie, a maintenance man on a four-wheeler passes me. He cuts off left through the grass, heading toward the soccer field where another maintenance man rides a mower, sending up the scent of fresh-cut grass.

A man on a mountain bike emerges from the trees on the right. Though it's a chilly April morning, he's wearing biking shorts and a form-fitted gray tank top. Through his amber-tinted athletic glasses, we make eye contact. I slow my pace, waving him on. He zips in front, then coasts the grassy hill down to the parking lot. A mixture of alcohol, dryer sheets, and cologne floats in his wake.

Strapped to my left arm just above the elbow, my phone rings. Without pausing, I glance at the number. I already wear wireless buds that emit only white noise—my choice for running.

I press the talk button. "Detective Brach here." It's a title I've had for six months now. I'm not sure I'll ever get tired of saying it.

"We've got a body."

TWO

FRESHLY SHOWERED with wet hair pulled into a ponytail, I drive my white Ford Interceptor up to the line of trees already sectioned off with yellow police tape. I slide from the SUV. Around my neck, I already wear my badge. Not that I need it. Most everyone in law enforcement here in White Quail, Tennessee—and the surrounding area—knows who I am.

At twenty-eight, I'm not only the youngest person to make detective in the county, but also the first woman.

Sheriff Owens catches my eye, waving me over. Early fifties, dark hair, ridiculously good-looking, and still resembling the quarterback he used to be when he went to high school with my mother. He took over the department when my grandfather, the former sheriff, passed away. Owens and I had a rocky start, but we've since developed a mutual respect.

Beside the sheriff stands a tall man in his early thirties.

Like me, he wears jeans, but that's where the similarity stops. Unlike my hiking shoes, his gray cowboy boots shine either with newness or a recent polish. And instead of my usual white windbreaker, an open black leather jacket shows a tucked-in gray shirt with a matching gray-striped tie. His badge sits secured at his waist to a leather belt. His brown hair has been combed and gelled into a slicked-back style.

I wonder how much wind it would take to un-slick it.

This must be the new detective Sheriff Owens said he'd be hiring.

The sheriff performs the introduction. "Detective Nell Brach meet Detective Vaughn London. He relocated here from Nashville. Today is his first official day."

Vaughn stands more than a head taller than me, which is saying something. At five-ten, not many men do. His hazel eyes crinkle with intellect and kindness as we shake hands. He wears just enough aftershave to not overpower.

"I've heard great things about you," he says.

"Thank you. I hope to live up to the accolades." I look toward the woods. "What do we have?"

Lifting the yellow tape, the sheriff leads the way. "Couple of boys called it in. They were playing this morning before school and found the body."

With a nod to a uniformed officer standing guard, we come to a stop. Surrounded by thick pines and partially covered by leaves, I stare down at the teenage girl. She lies curled on her side, her arms folded in front, dark hair matted with dirt, and blue eyes wide and glassy. She wears black leggings, one gray sneaker, and a long sleeve half-zip emerald-colored top. Scratches and bruising cover her face, neck, and hands.

"She's partially wet. It's not been raining," I say,

thinking about the area. "The rock quarry. It's on the other side of the woods."

Squatting down, Vaughn carefully studies her. "Jesus Christ, she's just a kid."

While he continues scrutinizing her, I pace away. The morning sun casts a prism of light. It dances as a gentle breeze stirs branches. About fifty yards east the woods give way to a neighborhood. The scent of breakfast meat floats through the air, smothered a bit by the nearby brewery. The faint sound of a baby crying trickles by.

Fifty yards. That's all she needed, and she would have gotten help.

"Anybody talk to the boys yet?" I ask. "Door to door? What about K9? Have you ordered a search of the quarry?"

"Leaving everything for you and Vaughn." Sheriff Owens walks to me. "You're the lead investigator on this one. Your first time. You ready?"

More than ready. I've been waiting for this. "Yes, sir." I give him a confident nod.

He hands me a small evidence bag with a credit card inside. "The boys who found her found this first while they were playing. Don't know if it's related."

I note the name Jack Macadem on the card. "Detective London, mind questioning the boys while I follow up with this card?"

"Call me Vaughn. And not a problem."

THREE

Monday, 9 a.m.

JACK MACADEM LIVES within the county, just over the city limit line of White Quail. I pull up in front of a powder blue two-story home situated on an acre of land. A trampoline and swing set sits to the right of the house, to the left a flower garden, and in front is one gray Honda Accord. An open garage door shows multiple bikes, neatly lined, shelves with toys and tools, and a work bench currently being used to stain a cabinet.

I step up onto the porch where two rocking chairs bracket in a round table decorated with a potted plant. The front door is propped open with a glass storm door closed. It offers a view straight back into a kitchen. A woman stands there, sliding cookies from a baking sheet onto a cooling rack.

I knock.

She jumps.

After wiping her hands on a hand towel, she walks the

short distance to greet me. Pretty and late thirties with curly dark hair, she opens the storm door. The sweet smell of sugar and cinnamon drifts out. Her blue eyes go straight to the badge hanging around my neck. Her flushed face pales.

She swallows. "Yes?"

"Ma'am, I'm Detective Nell Brach. Does Jack Macadem live here?"

Her hand tightens on the door. "Yes. Why? Oh, God, did something happen?"

"Are you Mrs. Macadem?"

She nods, jerkily. "Nina. You can call me Nina. Jack already left for work."

"Where does he work?"

"The brewery. Why, what's going on? Please tell me if he's okay."

"To my knowledge, yes, your husband is okay."

"What does that mean, to your knowledge?"

I nod past her into her home. "Why don't we speak inside?"

Nervously, she moves aside, showing me into a long living room with open French doors along the back that allow cool spring air in. Several feet in front of the French doors sit his and her powder-blue recliners with a table centered between them. On the table are two remotes and a glass bowl with wrapped candies.

"Let me just turn the oven off." She hurries away.

A paisley-patterned couch sits against the wall on the right with a coffee table in front. That coffee table's spindly legs wouldn't last a day around my house. My brother would prop his big feet on it and promptly break it.

Frankly, I would too.

An unlit fireplace is centered on the left wall with one framed photo on the mantel. It's a professional one, taken outdoors where everyone wears matching white shirts and jeans as they pose near a river. There's Nina and a muscular blond man who must be Jack. They have three girls—one teenager and elementary-aged twins, all with the mom's dark curly hair.

My attention narrows to the teenage girl and my stomach sours.

Behind me, a throat clears. "That's my family. Jack, Scarlett, and our twins."

Scarlett.

"Beautiful," I say.

"Thank you."

"You said your husband works at the brewery. Do you work?"

"Yes, part-time at the Catholic church. I'm a secretary."

"The one over on Main Street?"

"Yes."

"My grandparents went there."

She doesn't respond.

I turn fully to face her. "When was the last time you saw Scarlett?"

Tears rush to her eyes. "Why?"

"This morning?"

"No," she croaks. "Yesterday afternoon. Sh-she spent the night with her best friend. She's due home today after school." Tears blur her blue eyes, welling and tumbling over. "What's happened?"

FOUR

K9S SCURRY THROUGH THE WOODS, barking and sniffing. Vaughn stands, his back to the spot where Scarlett's body used to be, watching the dogs weave through the trees.

I step up beside him.

"That girl ran all over these woods, trying to get away," he says, without looking at me.

"Find anything?"

He holds up an evidence bag. "A torn piece of her shirt about twenty yards north, which is in the direction of the rock quarry. They hauled her off a few minutes ago." He begins walking in the wake of the dogs. I fall in step beside him. He says, "Soonest they can drag the quarry is this afternoon."

"I'll want to be here for that."

"Likewise. Also, I talked to the boys who found her. Other than being traumatized, neither offered anything of worth. It's as the sheriff said, they were playing before school and saw her. They ran for help. The parents called it in."

"Door to door?"

Vaughn nods. "A couple of our guys just started that."

"I believe her name is Scarlett Macadem. Jack, the credit card holder, is her father. I spoke with Nina Macadem, the mother. The last time they saw her was Sunday when she left to spend the night with a friend named Elle Psaltis. They're both eighth graders at the local junior high. I called the school. Elle is there. I'm heading that way next."

"If you don't mind, I'll come with you."

FIVE

I PULL my SUV into the junior high and park in a visitor spot. The brick school spans outward and up with the athletic fields to the left and behind it. Being the only junior high in the county, the classes are beyond capacity with overworked teachers and, unfortunately, overlooked students.

"This your alma mater?" Vaughn asks.

"No, I moved here when I was twenty-one. My brother, Tyler, goes here, though. He's in seventh grade. He should be in eighth, but he failed third grade. My mom went here as well but I think the place was just one or two buildings back then."

Bright morning sun beams down. I hold my hand up to block the rays.

Sniffing the air, Vaughn chuckles. "Tater tots. A school staple."

"You a ketchup or mustard tot kind of man?"

"Ketchup all the way. You?"

"Mustard, which you'll learn I eat on everything."

"Gross."

"Don't knock it until you try it." I open one of the many glass doors and step inside an overly warm corridor. To the right sits the administration area and I cut off, opening that glass door as well. I come to a stop when I see who is sitting outside the principal's office.

Almost as tall as me and with the same light hair and brown eyes, my brother sits slumped in a plastic chair two sizes too small for him. Nervously, his knee bounces as he stares at a spot on the beige carpet beneath his beat-up Nike running shoes.

"We were just about to call you," the secretary says as she rolls her eyes over to Tyler like I don't see him sitting there.

My brother glances up with a face full of shame. I know this can't be good, but my heart still squeezes. I walk over and sit down next to him. "What's going on?"

"I got caught smoking," he mumbles, barely able to maintain eye contact with me.

"Cigarettes?" I ask, hoping.

"Pot," he whispers.

I sigh.

The door to the principal's office opens. Dr. Gleason steps out. "Nell, we need to talk."

I stand, waving Vaughn over. "Dr. Gleason, this is Detective Vaughn London. We need to speak with us privately about another matter. Then we can address Tyler."

AFTER FILLING Dr. Gleason in on the body found who we believe is Scarlett Macadem, we request to speak with her friend, Elle Psaltis.

Elle arrives minutes later dressed in jogging pants, a school sweatshirt, and flip-flops. Chubby with straight shoulder-length black hair and pale skin, her movements are timid as she enters the principal's office.

We're already seated at a round table with five padded chairs. She chooses to sit right next to me, leaving the spot beside Vaughn open. From somewhere in the office, a sound machine emits a bubbling river that's meant to be tranquil. Instead, it annoys me.

After introductions are made, I ask her, "Do you know Scarlett Macadem?"

"She's my best friend."

"When was the last time you saw her?"

Elle's anxious gaze darts around the table. "Why?"

"How about you answer my question? When was the last time you saw her?"

"Sunday at the town carnival. She was supposed to go home with me, but she left with someone else. I told my mom she got sick and called her parents to come and get her. I was trying to cover for her." Elle cringes. "I'm going to be in so much trouble."

"Who did she leave with?"

"A boy." Under the table, Elle fidgets. "I thought I'd see her today. I was going to tell both of our parents this afternoon if Scarlett never showed up. I swear."

"The boy's name?"

"Um... I think his name is, um, Bennett Alexander. He goes to Fairview Academy. Ya know, that fancy private school?"

SIX

MY BEST FRIEND, Grace, and her husband, Matthew, live in a manufactured home on his family's farm. They moved here right after they married, going on six years now. Three kids later, Grace's dream of being a wife and mother suits her. Every time I see her, she's smiling.

Like now, as I pull up their long driveway, stopping in front of their crème-colored home with navy trim.

Off to the left, she kneels in a vegetable garden, picking kale and placing it in a basket. Her French braided red hair hangs halfway down her back. She wears her youngest in a baby Bjorn.

Laughing at something her three-year-old just said, Grace sees me and waves. Her five-year-old erupts from around the side of the house. With her hair also French braided, she's a miniature version of her mother, freckles and all.

"I don't know why you can't just take me home," Tyler

grumbles from the back seat. "I'm thirteen. I don't need a babysitter."

I catch my brother's disgruntled eye in the rearview. "Sure about that? Seems to me you get suspended from school, you need supervision." I look over to Vaughn sitting in the passenger side. "Be right back." To Tyler, I say, "Let's go."

Grace's five-year-old barrels into me as I close the driver's door. "Hiiiii."

"Hi, cutie." I hug her, smelling strawberries. "You smell yummy."

"It's berry-scented lip gloss." She purses her glossy lips. "Isn't it pretty?"

"It sure is."

Linking hands with me, she skips as I walk across the front yard toward Grace.

The three-year-old races past me, heading straight toward Tyler. Despite his grouchy mood, my brother smiles and ruffles the boy's hair.

Grace stays kneeling as I approach, but her interested gaze goes over to Vaughn still sitting in my vehicle. "Who's that?" she asks.

"My new partner. Detective Vaughn London. This is his first day. Moved here from Nashville."

"He's *cute*." She bounces her brows.

I roll my eyes. "Tyler got kicked out of school for smoking pot. Can I park him here for rest of the day? We've got a case I can't put on the back burner."

"What's pot?" the five-year-old asks.

"Something you are not allowed to do until you are much, *much* older," Grace answers her, then to me, loud enough for Tyler to hear, "I'll make sure to keep him *very* busy today."

By that, she means farm work plus babysitting the kids. The babysitting he never minds, but he hates the farm work. "Perfect," I say. "Thanks."

Back behind the wheel, I put the SUV in reverse.

"This your family?" Vaughn asks.

"Sort of. Grace and I go back a long way. Our mothers are best friends. Tyler and Luca, Grace's brother, are the same age as well."

"Tyler didn't seem too excited about being here."

"Tyler's not excited about anything these days."

"I was the same way at that age. Don't be too hard on him."

"Sometimes I don't think I'm hard enough."

Vaughn cuts me a curious look.

"Long story."

SEVEN

Monday, 1:15 p.m.

WE RUN THROUGH A PANERA DRIVE-THROUGH, both getting wraps—me chicken, with turkey for Vaughn.

"Where did you leave your vehicle?" I ask.

"At the station. I rode with Sheriff Owens to the woods this morning."

"What do you drive?"

"Currently a Mini Cooper." He holds up a hand. "Don't ask."

I laugh. "We'll be using my vehicle then."

"Agreed."

A call comes in from the coroner. "We confirmed the body is Scarlett Macadem. We'll need one of the parents for a final ID."

Though I already knew the dead girl would be Scarlett Macadem, actually hearing the words weighs deep in my chest. "Okay, we'll let the family know."

I make myself take a bite of lunch. It tastes like paste.

A text comes in letting us know they started dragging the quarry.

We eat and drive the rest of the way in silence.

Several vehicles jam the area leading into the quarry—a Jeep, a cop car, a two-door fire department truck, and a van. By the time we park behind everyone else and walk through the open gate, a crane is pulling a tan Nissan Sentra from the deep, clear water. Two men and one woman stand in a clump, all dressed in blue and white diving gear, representing county rescue. A uniformed officer hovers nearby, watching as well.

I eye the progress as Vaughn paces the quarry that looks to be the size of a football field. Giant boulders line the water built up on one side by rubble. I look to the south where the rubble ends and trees begin, leading into the woods where Scarlett ran. I see no buildings, only the crane currently in use and a dump truck full of small rocks.

Vaughn returns. "I saw charred ground from a fire. Probably kids hanging out. This isn't in use anymore. The local brewery now owns the land. No one monitors it. That crane is left over from when the quarry was last in use, just six months ago."

"You were gone for five minutes. How did you learn all that?"

He motions over to the dump truck where a man dressed in all khaki stands. "He works at the brewery. Was driving home and stopped to see what was going on. The van belongs to him."

The crane pauses mid-air, slowly swinging the tan four-door Nissan to shore. Water pours from it as they carefully lower it to a flat area. Vaughn calls the tag in. We slip on latex gloves.

All four windows are halfway down. It would've filled with water fairly quickly.

I peek into the back area, seeing a child's seat fastened in, a gray blanket, and a pink and white backpack—all partially submerged in water. On the other side of the car, Vaughn flicks on a flashlight. His beam picks up one floating gray sneaker, its lace caught in the corner nearest me.

"Scarlett was wearing the other one," I say.

I open the back. Water pours out. It's then I see it—on the door's interior—indentations and scratch marks. Anger creeps through me. She kicked and clawed her way free.

A torn piece of emerald-colored fabric is stuck in the crease of the window that's rolled halfway down. That's probably how Scarlett finally got out.

My partner's phone buzzes with a text. Quickly, he reads it. "Car belongs to one Ronan Aaron. Know him?"

Yes.

"He's a judge," I say.

He's also my lover.

In my periphery, I spy a muscular blond man charging across the quarry. The uniformed officer moves to intercede, but the man shoves past.

"Where is she?" he yells. "Where is my daughter?"

EIGHT

Monday, 3 p.m.

VAUGHN and I stand outside the mortuary. A few feet away, Mr. Macadem presses his forehead into the white wall, rocking slightly, his eyes tightly closed. The hallway yawns indefinitely under the hospital. At the end, a door opens. Mrs. Macadem steps through.

Already sobbing, she stumbles and runs toward her husband. They collide. Gripping each other tightly, their grief echoes along the corridor.

My stomach cinches tight. Seven years ago, this could have been me and Mom. It almost was.

The door to the mortuary opens. The elderly coroner doesn't speak, she simply makes eye contact with me, nodding, silently letting me know Scarlett's ready.

———

AT THE POLICE STATION, I now sit across from Mr. Macadem. In the room beside us, Vaughn is speaking with Mrs. Macadem.

"Mr. Macadem, do I have your consent to record our conversation?"

Without looking at me, he nods.

Beside me, a camera sits mounted on a tripod. I press record. "When was the last time you saw Scarlett?"

With his large hands clasped tightly on the table between us, he doesn't make eye contact with me. Instead, he stares at his knuckles, popping white with a lack of circulation. "Sunday. We just got home from Mass. I was in the garage. She was standing right beside me, watching me stain our new kitchen cabinets."

"Did she say anything?"

"No, we're a lot alike that way. She's a quiet girl. Unlike her sisters who babble constantly. Scarlett and I, we...we just hang out." His head tilts up. His gaze, heavy with grief, meets mine. "Ya know?"

I nod. "You were in the garage, then what?"

"Then Elle and her mom showed up. 'Bye Daddy,' Scarlett said." His voice cracks. He looks back to his cinched fingers. He sniffs. "She got in their car and left."

"Did she have anything with her?"

"Her backpack because she was staying the night."

"Did you know she had your credit card?"

"Yeah, I gave it to her earlier because I didn't have any cash. I wanted her to have fun."

"Where were they going?"

"The town carnival. Then the girls were sleeping over at Elle's. Scarlett was due back home today after school."

"Is it normal for your thirteen-year-old daughter and her friend to go places unsupervised?"

Mr. Macadem's eyes snap to mine. His grief transitions to a scowl. "All the kids around here go to that carnival when it comes to town. They're thirteen, not five."

"Of course." Gently, I nod. The last thing I want is for him to be on the defensive with me. "Does Scarlett have a boyfriend?"

"No." His eyes widen. "Why?"

"I have to ask. What about extracurricular activities? Does she ever go to the courthouse?"

"Y-yes. How did you know that?"

"Is that part of school?"

He nods. "She's taking a high school government class. It's part of that. Elle does, too, as well as several other eighth graders."

"Do you know anything about the rock quarry? Does Scarlett hang out there?"

Slowly, his thick fingers unclasp. His hands disappear under the table. "Detective Brach, Scarlett is a good girl. She makes great grades. She's sweet and kind, quiet and reserved. She doesn't do things like hanging out at rock quarry and partying. Because that's what you're getting at, right?"

"The only thing I'm getting at is the truth. I have to ask questions. Please don't interpret them as anything else."

Several long seconds thump by. Mr. Macadem keeps staring at me. Quietly, I maintain eye contact that I hope shows the compassion I feel. He needs to understand I'm not the bad person here. I truly want to help. I am on Scarlett's side.

"I held her hand, at the mortuary." His thick neck rolls with a swallow. "Why were her fingers so torn up?"

Because she clawed her way from the back of a car that belongs to my lover. But of course, I don't say that or anything. I can't until we receive an official report from forensics.

"We're figuring that out," I assure him.

Mr. Macadem's hands reappear, clasping behind his wide neck as he blows out a long breath. "You will find who did this."

I want nothing more than to make promises to this devastated father. Yet, I can't. "I will do my best," I respond.

"No, you will find who did this."

NINE

Monday, 5:15 p.m.

SWEET RIVER IS a small town west of White Quail known for Fairview Academy, an elite all-boys boarding school that caters to students from all over the world. Other than the academy, a mom-and-pop grocery store, a gas station, and one restaurant that serves breakfast only, Sweet River is a blink-and-you-miss-it town.

An open, wrought iron gate leads up a long, paved drive bordered by manicured lawns. To the right, a stable with an equestrian ring takes up a half-acre of land. Next comes a lacrosse field, followed by a gymnasium. The drive curves around multiple two-story brick buildings, leading to a back lot full of vehicles that cost more than my annual salary.

Vaughn whistles.

Being the end of the school day, high school boys filter from buildings, most dressed in athletic clothes. I park in a guest spot.

More brick buildings surround a common area.

Together, Vaughn and I tread across, weaving through clumps of boys, and head toward a door marked DEAN OF STUDENTS.

I'd called ahead, so when we walk in, the dean is already waiting with Bennett Alexander, the boy Scarlett left the carnival with.

With artfully messy sandy brown hair, he sits slumped at a round table in the dean's office, scrolling through his phone. He looks so much older than Scarlett.

"Put your phone down," the dean says.

An exasperated, dramatic sigh fills the air. Bennett puts his phone facedown on the tabletop. Then he smacks his lips as he looks up at us through bored, brown eyes.

Normally, I would sit, making the atmosphere comfortable and full of trust. However, I remain standing. This boy hasn't said a word, but I already don't like his disrespectful body language. He needs to know I'm the one in charge.

Vaughn follows my lead, standing to my right.

"Sit up," I say.

With another sigh, this one even more loud and annoyed, he does what I request.

"Bennett Alexander?" I ask.

"Yeah."

"Do you know Scarlett Macadem?"

He smirks. "Yeah."

"When was the last time you saw her?"

"Sunday."

"Where was this?"

Another smirk. "Back seat of my car where I popped her cherry."

"Mr. Alexander!" the dean explodes. "That is uncalled for."

"Is she your girlfriend?" Vaughn asks, his tone measured and much more cool-tempered than I feel.

Bennett snorts. "She wishes."

The door to the dean's office bangs open. An angry man with gray hair railroads in.

"Mr. Alexander," the dean says. "We call—"

Mr. Alexander holds a hand up, shutting the dean down. He snaps his fingers at Bennett. "Get up."

The boy takes his time sliding his phone from the table and standing.

Swinging a finger into my face, Mr. Alexander barks, "You want to talk to my son? You call my lawyer." He slaps a business card down on the table and glares at the dean as Bennett walks right past me, sneering.

When the door closes, I force myself to calmly pick up the lawyer's card. "I didn't realize some of your students are from local families," I say, looking at the dean.

"Only Bennett. He lives here at the school, but his dad lives over in White Quail. He owns the brewery."

TEN

Monday, 6 p.m.

THE LAST HOUR of sunlight clings to the sky as we pull into the police station. I park right next to a Mini Cooper. "Cute," I say.

Vaughn jokingly glowers.

A text comes in.

Grace: It's date night tonight. I dropped Tyler off at Mom's place. Hope that's okay?
Me: Of course. Thanks for watching him.
Grace: Any time.

Vaughn notes the messages. "Need to go home?"

"Soon, yeah. Olivia, that's Grace's mother, never minds helping out. Luca and Tyler, though, don't get along. It wears on Olivia. I don't like to outstay the welcome."

"Luca being Grace's brother, right?"

"Yes. Those boys were inseparable as kids, but the older

they get, the more they seem to detest each other. They even got in a fistfight a few months back."

We step from my vehicle.

"Sounds like me and my brother. So many fights over the years."

I hadn't thought of it from that angle, but perhaps Vaughn has a point. It's more of a brother-bicker thing. At least I hope so. Our two families are forever intertwined. I don't want the boys to hate each other.

"What about your parents?" Vaughn asks, opening the door to the station.

"Oh, now, what kind of detective are you if you can't figure out my backstory."

"A challenge." He smiles.

Sheriff Owens steps from his office when he sees us crossing over the workroom to our face-fronting desks. He hands us a folder with S. *Macadem Forensics* penciled on the tab. "I just printed this."

"Already?"

"Slow day."

As Owens walks back into his office, I open the folder. The sheriff made copies, and after giving Vaughn his set, I lean against my desk and peruse.

"She was a virgin," Vaughn notes.

"So much for Bennett 'popping her cherry.'"

"He's a little dick."

"That he is."

We continue reading. I note the time of death Sunday at 11 p.m. "Cause of death: secondary drowning." Silently, I read the comments on that term. *Not common. Occurs after being in the water where fluid has built up in the lungs.*

Vaughn says, "She was definitely in the back of Ronan Aaron's car."

"And tried to claw her way out."

"Bruising on her ribs that match the window, consistent with how she finally escaped. Miscellaneous bruising and scratches from running in the woods." Vaughn folds his papers lengthwise.

"DNA from the woods is all over the place. Footprints too. Given the neighborhood kids play in that area, that's understandable." I close the folder, taking a peek at my watch.

"Got time to question Judge Aaron?" Vaughn asks.

"Let me text Olivia. Shouldn't be a problem. However, do me a favor and take lead when we get to the judge's office."

Vaughn's brows arch up. "Anything I should know?"

"Nope, just need you to take lead."

ELEVEN

Monday, 7:15 p.m.

WE DRIVE SEPARATELY to the courthouse so that I can
go home directly after. I don't bother calling ahead. Ronan
will be there. He's a late-to-work, late-to-leave type of man.

At this hour, plenty of empty parking spaces are open in
front of the brick and stone courthouse that is situated in
White Quail's historical town square. Three stories with
towering white columns and multiple round balconies, it
looks more like a plantation mansion than a government
building. Maybe it once was.

Vaughn follows me up the wide stone steps and through
the double front doors. We make quick work of security
check before taking a curved stairwell to the second floor.
His boots click on the polished hardwood. My hiking shoes
make no sound.

We pass an empty courtroom, a closed vehicle registra-
tion office, and a row of padded benches, all empty.

Around a corner and down another hall brings us to

Judge Ronan Aaron's chambers. The exterior thick mahogany door sits propped open with a fan on and directed at the secretary's desk. I step around the box fan. Vaughn follows.

"Hey, Nell," Ophelia, Ronan's secretary greets me. She just turned seventy but looks like she's ten years younger. She's worked here at the courthouse since she was a teenager. I asked her once if she ever planned on retiring and she scoffed, saying, "Lord, I'd be so bored."

I'm way off from retirement, but I already know I'd be bored as well.

"Ophelia, this is my new partner, Detective Vaughn London."

With perfectly coiffed black hair and makeup as fresh as if it was this morning, Ophelia stands. She holds out a hand to shake. "Welcome. I heard the sheriff hired a new guy."

"Glad to be here," Vaughn says.

I look toward the matching mahogany door that leads into Ronan's office. "Is he in?"

"Yes." She crosses over and knocks. "Judge Aaron, do you have a moment for Detective Brach?"

A long pause follows. "Send her in," he finally calls out.

I hate that his deep voice gives me butterflies.

Ronan's twenty years my senior. We met several years ago when I was still a uniformed officer and had to appear in his court for a traffic stop. We met again weeks later at a 5k race in town. Then again at a bar-b-que fundraiser. The fourth time our paths crossed, we ended up in bed together. And that has been our relationship going on for four years now.

No one knows. Not even my best friend, Grace.

Ophelia opens the door and steps aside. I enter first,

followed by Vaughn. Ronan's handsome smile fades when he sees my partner trailing behind.

"If you're good, I'm going to head home for the evening," Ophelia says.

Ronan waves her off. "Sure thing, see you tomorrow."

With a shaved head, deep blue eyes, and a lean runner's build, Ronan rolls his high-back leather chair out and stands. Dressed in a white polo shirt with navy slacks, he steps around his vast desk.

"Judge Ronan Aaron, this is my new partner, Detective Vaughn London."

Standing eye to eye, the two men shake hands.

Ronan looks between us. "Everything okay?"

"Mind if we sit for a few minutes?" I motion to the two padded leather chairs situated in front of his desk.

Ronan nods, retaking his seat as Vaughn and I take ours.

I nod to my partner, letting him know he should proceed. Vaughn shows Ronan a photo of the tan Nissan. "Does this car belong to you?"

He spares it a glance. "Yes. Why is it at the rock quarry?"

"We were hoping you could answer that," Vaughn says.

Ronan shrugs. "I don't know. I have four vehicles. I don't drive that one."

"Who does?"

"My nanny. Is he okay?"

"Who is your nanny?" Vaughn asks.

"Gerald Macadem. He lives in my garage apartment."

Ronan's a widower with a six-year-old son. I knew he had a nanny named Gerald but I didn't know the last name. Now though I jot it down.

Vaughn also notes it. "Any relation to Jack and Nina Macadem?"

"Yes, Gerald and Jack are brothers." Ronan looks between us again. "What's going on?"

"Do you know Scarlett Macadem?" my partner asks next.

"That's Jack and Nina's girl. Yes, I know her."

"From where? Through your nanny?"

"Yes, she sometimes hangs out with her uncle at my place. So do the twins, Scarlett's younger sisters. I have a big pool they swim in. Also, Scarlett comes here with her classmates."

"Where were you last night?"

"At home with my son."

"Where was your nanny, Gerald Macadem?"

"He had the weekend off. He told me he was going camping with a friend."

"When was the last time you saw Gerald?"

"Saturday morning before he left for the weekend."

"You haven't seen him today?"

"No, I sleep late. He gets my son up and ready for school. I'll see them both when I go home in a few minutes."

Ronan shifts forward in his chair, looking at me now. Confusion mars his gaze. "Please tell me what's going on."

Tamping down the urge to comfort him, I look away and over to my partner who says, "Scarlett Macadem was found dead this morning in the woods next to the rock quarry. Before that, she was in your car at the bottom of the quarry."

———

AS I DRIVE HOME, rapid-fire texts from Ronan come.

Ronan: I don't have anything to do with this.

Ronan: You have to believe me.

Ronan: Why didn't you speak while you were in my office?

Ronan: Why aren't you responding to my texts?

Ronan: Can we talk?

Ronan: Nell...?

With each one, my heart hurts more and more. I pull into my neighborhood of small homes, drive the short distance to our brown-painted three-bedroom/one-bath, and park in our driveway which is in dire need of resurfacing. In the side yard sits Grandpa's '65 short-bed Chevy that I don't have the heart to sell.

I send Olivia a text.

Me: I'm home, send Tyler on over.

Oliva and Luca live in the adjacent neighborhood, separated from ours by a wall of trees. A passageway cut through the trees allows residents to easily move back and forth. I keep my eyes on the pass-through for Tyler as I text Ronan.

Me: I need to stay removed from you during this investigation. All communication will go through Vaughn. I know you understand. Please stop texting me.

I hit send, already dreading tomorrow. I'm going to have to tell Sheriff Owens. The last thing I need is this coming back around to slap me across the face.

With a backpack slung over one shoulder and carrying Tupperware, Tyler steps through the trees. He spies me getting out of my vehicle and waves. I'm glad to see the wave. Now if I could just get a smile.

At the front door, Tyler shows me the Tupperware. "Olivia sent beef and broccoli for dinner."

"Perfect."

"Is Scarlett Macadem dead?"

"Yes, how do you know that?"

He holds up his phone. "It's all over Insta."

"Which you're grounded from by the way." I take the phone from his fingers as I step into our house. I scroll his feed, seeing mostly RIP posts with pictures of Scarlett and her pretty smile.

Tyler throws his backpack onto the worn, brown-plaid couch—yet something else in dire need of replacement. He walks into the kitchen with its cracked linoleum and snags a juice box from the refrigerator. He drinks it down in one insanely long swallow.

After a burp, he says, "Does this have anything to do with The Quiet Game?"

TWELVE

Tuesday, 8:45 a.m.

I DROP Tyler off with Grace, then drive to the station. Sheriff Owens is leaving as I pull in.

"Sheriff, we need to speak."

"Later. I'm due in court." He jumps in his blue sheriff's car and speeds away.

Inside, Vaughn's already at our desks. Dressed in jeans, a tucked-in white shirt with a Miss Piggy tie, and those polished gray cowboy boots, he's frowning as he reads something on his phone.

I put my stuff down. "Everything okay?"

"Yeah." He places the phone face down on the desk. "Just something going on back home." He forces a smile. "Good morning."

"Good morning." I look closer at his tie. "Cute."

"Yesterday was my formal striped-tie day. From here on out, this is what you get. It's my way of disarming people." He smiles.

"I like."

He hands me a large coffee.

Gladly, I accept. "You're handy to have around." I sip. "With coconut milk? How'd do you know?"

"Excellent detective skills." The corners of his lips curve with an empathetic smile. "I'm sorry about what happened with your brother, his friend Luca, and your mom. That's a lot for you to take on."

When my brother and Luca were six, they were taken and almost killed. I was just a cadet then and broke about every law out there to find them. When I located their kidnapper I beat him so viciously that he died. It was not self-defense. I had more than overpowered him.

Mom saw the whole thing. Before I knew what was happening, she took the blame. She told the cops that she delivered the brutal and murderous bludgeoning. Thanks to Sheriff Owens, Mom was sentenced to the best mental hospital in the area instead of prison. Her taking the fall for me is a secret only three people know: me, Mom, and Sheriff Owens.

Up until that point I had always viewed her as fragile and weak. Now, I owe her my life.

"More excellent detective skills?" I joke, trying to lighten the mood.

Silently, Vaughn nods, accepting I don't want to talk about this. "Thought we'd start with Gerald Macadem?"

"Actually, we need to go to Fairview Academy. I'll tell you about The Quiet Game on the way."

THIRTEEN

Tuesday, 10 a.m.

"THIS SOUNDS like something out of a movie." Through his gunmetal-framed Ray Bans, Vaughn glances over at me. "Kids are recruited to play this insane game where they earn points and bragging rights to being, what, the county jackass?"

I turn on my blinker, then pull through the open iron gate of Fairview Academy. "That's what Tyler said. It's a high school thing, but some middle schoolers get chosen to participate. Tyler's never been approached and he doesn't know if it's a real thing, but he's heard the rumors. There's supposed to be an abandoned building on the academy's property where it takes place. Maybe it starts there and extends out to other areas, like the rock quarry."

"Kids are idiots."

"Agreed."

I pull into the same guest spot as yesterday and park. I didn't call ahead. The dean stands in the common area speaking with two boys dressed in burgundy school jackets and tan pants. The dean glances up as we climb from my vehicle. With a goodbye to the students, he walks straight toward us.

"Sir." I shake his hand. "Is there an abandoned building on this property?"

FAIRVIEW ACADEMY'S property encompasses one hundred acres. The north side of the grounds borders a forest. On that border sits a one-story, thousand-square-foot concrete building covered in mildew, poison ivy, and more than one rogue vine.

The dean fishes for a key on his ring. "Our groundskeeper uses this for storage."

"What was it before?" I ask.

"Always been storage."

"When was the last time you were out here?"

"Years, I think."

I note a dirt road cut through the bordering trees with a closed and locked gate. An attached sign says PRIVATE PROPERTY. Where does that go?"

"Connects over to the highway." The dean unlocks the rusted metal door on the concrete building.

"Stay here, please." I step into a small dark hallway smelling of fertilizer, cigarettes, and mold. It's an odd combination. Overhead, a chain dangles from one single bulb. Vaughn pulls the string. The bulb flicks to bright white.

From my windbreaker, I take out a pair of latex gloves and snap them on. Vaughn does the same. There are two closed doors—one immediately to our right, and the other further down the narrow hall. Vaughn turns the knob on the first door. It swings inward. A window covered by foliage lets in intermittent light to show shelves full of bags, bottles, and boxes—all related to gardening. The pungent smell singes my nostrils. A plastic Adirondack chair occupies one corner with a blue cooler beside it. Inside the cooler is a six-pack of warm domestic beer.

I lead the way down the hall to the next door. Like the first one, it swings inward. Unlike the first room, black paint covers the window, cloaking the room in darkness. The smell of cigarettes and alcohol hangs heavy. Overhead dangles one bulb with an attached chain. When I pull it, a dim-yellow glow fans out.

"Oh my God," Vaughn mutters.

A twin-sized mattress covered in a striped blue and white sheet occupies the corner with blood in the center. A tripod and camera have been set up against the back wall, pointed at the mattress. Several ashtrays litter the floor, full of cigarette butts and joint roaches. A cardboard box near the mattress holds liquor bottles—some empty, some still full. On the concrete wall behind the mattress are tick marks—some red, some white—next to initials, like a scoreboard.

Ten initials, all written in black.

An empty soup can beside the mattress holds the Sharpie pens used on the wall.

"I'll call it in," Vaughn says, backing out of the room.

I stay where I am, staring at the wall. From my front jeans pocket, I take out my car keys with an attached pen light. I flip it on, stepping closer.

Directing the beam at the tick marks, I gently touch a red one with my latex-covered index finger.

That's not Sharpie. That's blood.

FOURTEEN

Tuesday, noon

WITH A UNIFORMED OFFICER IN PLACE, the building secure, and waiting on county forensics to arrive, Vaughn and I hunt down the groundskeeper.

Sixty-five years old with thin gray hair, ten functional teeth, and carrying most of his weight in his gut, Charlie Duncan hunches over a bush near the equestrian area, pulling weeds.

"Charlie Duncan?" I ask, ignoring the plumber's crack peeking out from his green pants.

Over his shoulder and through bloodshot, glassy eyes, he looks at me. "Yeah?"

I flash my badge. "I'm Detective—"

He takes off running, or more like stumbling.

Vaughn sighs. "Of course, he's going to be an issue." With two giant steps, my partner snags the older man by the flabby upper arm and pushes him facedown into the lush grass.

"Git off me!" Charlie screams.

Planting his knee into the gardener's back, Vaughn puts a firm hand on the side of Charlie's head. "You can behave and talk with us here or I can put you in cuffs and haul you to the station. Thoughts?"

Charlie squirms. "Fine! Jeez!"

"You'll behave?" Vaughn asks.

"Yeah. Yeah."

"Okay, I'm letting you go." My partner releases him and stands.

Charlie rolls over, but he doesn't get up. He stays seated in the grass, glowering up at us. "What?"

I squat down to his level. "Where were you Sunday night?"

"Passed out drunk."

"Something tells me you spend a lot of nights passed out drunk."

"Whad of it?" He sniffs, wiping one hairy hand under his nose.

"Can anyone confirm this?" I ask.

He laughs, showing gap-toothed gums. "Guess you didn't do yuns homework. I was sleepin' it off in one of your cells."

Vaughn folds his arms. "Tell us about the abandoned building where you keep your surplus supplies, beer...and the room with the mattress."

Charlie's flushed cheeks pale. With a disappointed sigh, he plucks a handful of grass and tosses it. "One good thang in my life and you found it. Well, shit."

I lean in, my voice lowers. "What goes on in that room?"

"Boys 'round here have a competition going, bangin' the local girls. Even got differ colored marks on the wall for virgins or not. Extra points fer the ones they film. It ain't rape. The girls give consent. Believe me, I'd do something if it was rape."

"How noble of you," Vaughn murmurs.

"How do you know all of this?" I ask.

"They send me the videos in exchange for my keepin' thangs quiet."

"Where are these videos?" I ask.

"Latest one's on my phone. Why?"

I hold a hand out.

With a scowl, Charlie slides his cell from his back pocket and slaps it into my palm. "I better git that back."

"What do you know about The Quiet Game?"

"I ain't never heard of it."

"Was there a girl in that room over the weekend?"

"Yeah."

On his phone, Vaughn brings up a photo of Scarlett. "This her?"

Charlie takes the cell, pinching it to zoom in. "Nah, it was some fat virgin with black hair. That be the video on my phone that you just cons-fis-cated." Charlie clears his throat, swallowing the snot instead of spitting it out. "That it? Can I go now?"

"No." I reach for him. "You're under arrest."

"For what?"

"We'll start with child pornography and go from there."

FIFTEEN

AT THE STATION, we hand Charlie off.

The uniformed officer working at the front desk says, "Gerald Macadem is in Room Two waiting. He came in on his own. Been here for hours. I told him it might be a while and he seemed content to wait."

"Thank you. Next time feel free to let me know." I pause, glancing up at the TV mounted in the lobby. It shows Judge Aaron coming down the courthouse steps.

A reporter rushes him. "What is your response to Scarlett Macadem?"

He almost misses a step. "My heart goes out to the family."

"Why was Scarlett in the back of a vehicle registered to you?"

"No comment." He sidesteps the reporter and hurries to his sports car parked along the curb.

I turn away from the TV and look at Vaughn. "Considering we haven't made a statement, someone said something." I hand him Charlie's phone. "Why don't you get started with this and I'll talk to Gerald Macadem."

With a nod, Vaughn walks through the door that leads to the back of the station. I follow, cutting off down the hall toward the interrogation rooms, where I find Gerald Macadem, a younger version of his blond, muscular brother, Jack.

Nervously, his leg bounces as he picks at his thumbnail. When I walk in, he looks up. "Detective Brach?" he asks.

"Yes." I pull out a metal chair opposite him and sit down. "Thank you for coming in."

"Judge Aaron said I should. Also, I would've anyway. I can't believe Scarlett's dead. Mr. Aaron told me last night when he got home from work. I immediately called my brother. He could barely talk. I'm going over there after I finish here. I feel horrible about this. I should've told Mr. Aaron the car was gone." His eyes close. "Oh God, my poor brother."

"Why don't we take a breath? Would you like some water?"

His eyes open back up. "No."

"Do I have your consent to record our conversation?"

"Yes."

Beside me stands the tripod and camera. I can't help but think of another tripod and camera as I press the record button. "Where were you this weekend?"

"I had Saturday and Sunday off. I went camping and fishing with a friend of mine. I'll give you his name and number."

"That would be great. Thank you."

"He drove and dropped me off Sunday night around nine at my place. I live in the garage apartment on Judge Aaron's property. I hadn't had a shower all weekend and needed one. I put all my gear in the garage. The car was there when I did. I went up to my apartment and took a very long shower. Then I grabbed a beer and kicked back on the couch until I fell asleep. When I woke up the next morning I was still on the couch. I got up and around, went downstairs, and that's when I realized the car was gone. Mr. Aaron was still sleeping. I don't know. I guess I figured the housekeeper borrowed it. Sometimes she does that if her car is giving her problems. Mr. Aaron doesn't mind. Honestly, I didn't think anything about it. There's a car seat in the truck as well, so I used that one for the day."

"Where are the vehicles parked?"

"He has two garages. A secure one connected to the house and a separate one that's open-aired. I live above the open-aired one. The Nissan and the truck are kept in that one. The sports car and the Jeep—those are what Ronan drives—he keeps in the secure garage."

"Where are the keys to the Nissan and truck kept?"

"On a wall unit in the open-aired garage."

I've never been to Ronan's home, but I know where he lives. It's not gated and though his house sits way back from the main road, anyone could walk up and straight into that garage. "Are there security cameras on the property?"

"There used to be. Ronan's in the process of upgrading them."

WHEN I STEP from Room Two, a uniformed officer approaches handing me a white eight-by-ten envelope. "Security print from the town carnival on Sunday."

"Thanks." As I walk to find Vaughn, I slide the photo

from the envelope. It clearly shows both girls—Elle and Scarlett—climbing into Bennett Alexander's Land Rover.

The men's restroom door opens. Sheriff Owens emerges. He glances at the photo, time-stamped Sunday afternoon. "Mr. Macadem called me directly and left a message. He wants to know how Scarlett died and why she was in Judge Aaron's vehicle. Between his brother Gerald and what he's seeing on the news, Mr. Macadem is getting all kinds of information. You need to get over to their house and give him what answers you can."

"I will. I also need to speak with you privately when you have a chance."

"Everything okay?"

"I think so. I would like to carve out time today, though. It can't wait."

"Please don't tell me you're resigning."

"No, of course not." I keep walking down the hall. The sheriff falls in step beside me. "We have a video Vaughn is watching," I say. "I want to see what's on it before the next steps."

"I was heading there myself."

When I open the door to the incident room, a girl's whimper filters from the laptop speakers. My stomach clenches. Face grim, Vaughn pauses the video. He turns the laptop to give us a better view. He presses rewind, then play.

A hand comes into view, moving away from the camera. Elle Psaltis sits cross-legged in the center of the mattress, looking nervously at the wall of tick marks. With only his back visible, a boy walks over to the box of liquor and selects whiskey. He unscrews the top and drinks. He offers the bottle to Elle. She accepts, drinking. She coughs. He takes the bottle back, drinking more. Then her again, this time not coughing.

He leaves her holding the bottle as he kneels on the mattress, finally coming into view. It's Bennett Alexander. He holds up a joint, smiling. Nodding, she smiles as well. He lights it, taking and holding a puff. He gives the joint to her. She mimics him, inhaling and holding. Together, they blow out. They each go again, coughing on the second round. They laugh. They take turns with the whiskey.

One more round of the joint before Bennett places it on top of an already full ashtray. He turns back right as Elle hugs him—laughing, laughing, laughing.

"Shh," he says, giggling. "Remember, we're supposed to be quiet."

"Shh," she agrees, pursing her lips and placing an index finger on them.

They kiss. They roll around. They laugh some more. She lifts her knee-length cotton skirt, flashing panties with yellow daisies. Bennett reaches for the underwear. Clumsily, he gets them down her legs. From his front jeans pocket, he brings out a condom. Her eyes widen as she watches him undo his jeans and lower them before rolling the condom on.

Her laughter dies. She swallows.

He stays kneeling, his penis erect, staring at her like he's waiting on something. Finally, he throws his hands up. "I don't get the point unless you consent and turn around. So?"

Elle's nervous gaze flicks to the camera. Her lips wobble into a hesitant smile. She nods, consenting, before turning on all fours. Bennett doesn't wait. He enters her fast and hard. She whimpers.

"Shh," he grunts.

Three thrusts and he's done.

He pulls out. Blood smears the condom that he snaps off and shoves down in his back pocket. He zips up his jeans. Elle turns over, resuming her cross-legged spot on the mattress. She stares at her right bare knee as he takes a red Sharpie to create a tick mark next to his initials: **BA**. He's now got six tick marks—three white and three red—more than anybody else. After recapping the pen, he turns to Elle and holds out a hand.

Ignoring his offer, she climbs from the mattress. Bennett notes the blur of blood on the blue and white sheet. Leaning down, he picks up her yellow daisy underwear and hands them to her. As he walks toward the camera, I keep my eyes on Elle. She reaches up and under her cotton skirt. With a wince, she brings out a bloody middle finger. She studies it as Bennett fumbles with the camera.

A few seconds go by.

She looks over her shoulder at him, but he's scowling into the lens and not paying her attention.

Elle gives the camera her back. Her hand comes up, moving toward the wall. Then she traces the bloody middle finger down the red sharpie mark Bennett made.

The screen goes black.

I have to force myself to unclench my teeth. As much as I hate admitting it, I say, "That video has nothing to do with Scarlett." I toss the photo from the school carnival onto the table in front of Vaughn. "But this does. Time stamps prove she was with them one hour before that video got made. I need to go talk to the Macadem family. Can you handle Bennett and Elle?"

"I'm on it." Vaughn stands.

SIXTEEN

Tuesday, 3 p.m.

AFTER LEAVING my partner with the task of tracking down Bennett Alexander and Elle Psaltis, I snag a PowerBar from my desk drawer. I'd totally forgotten to eat lunch. As I hungrily take the first bite, I walk from the station toward my vehicle.

I know exactly how the conversation is going to go with the boy and his daddy's lawyer. *It wasn't rape. She consented. You saw. According to the Romeo and Juliet law, you have nothing here.*

These boys take girls in that disgusting room thinking they're so clever with that consent angle. They know which girls to target. I've had one encounter with Elle and she came across as nervous, timid, and lacking confidence. She's on the outside looking in, likely bullied, and wants to belong but doesn't know how.

Christ, she's the same age as my little brother.

"Nell?"

I pause. Ronan walks toward me. *Shit.* He does not look happy. He comes to a stop well within my personal space—so close his aftershave surrounds us.

"We can't be talking," I say.

Ronan clasps my upper arm a little too firmly. I don't look up into his face. Instead, I look at his fingers around my arm. He takes the hint and releases his hold.

"Have you seen the front page of the paper?" he snaps. "Do you know I'm on the news? Just this morning, a reporter railroaded me outside the courthouse." His voice lowers, becoming angrier. "Who the hell released my name?"

"I don't know."

"Well, what are you going to do about it?"

"Nothing. I have a dead girl to solve."

He steps even closer, his voice lower still. "That isn't good enough."

"What do you want, Judge Aaron?"

"I want you to arrest someone."

"Detective Brach?" Sheriff Owens calls out.

Ronan takes a step back. From across the station's lot, my eyes meet the sheriff's. I don't have to say a word. He now knows what I need to speak to him about.

———

AS I'M DRIVING across town to talk with Mr. and Mrs. Macadem, my phone rings.

"Sheriff," I answer the call.

"Three things."

"Okay."

"One, are you his alibi?"

"No."

"Two, you will keep things professional with him until this is over."

"Yes."

"Three, this is you officially notifying your superior, *me*, that you are romantically involved with Judge Ronan Aaron."

"Yes."

"Then there is no reason to remove you from the case."

"Thank you, Sheriff."

SEVENTEEN

Tuesday, 3:30 p.m.

IN THE MACADEM HOME, I sit at the kitchen table across from Jack and Nina. When I arrived, Gerald was already here. I asked him for privacy and he's now outside leaning up against the truck that belongs to Ronan Aaron.

I look first at Nina's splotchy face and then into Jack's stoic eyes. "I know you're being railroaded from several angles right now. I'd like to make sure you have all the correct information that I'm allowed to say."

"Are you allowed to tell us how she died?" Mr. Macadem asks.

"I am. It was secondary drowning. It's when a person inhales water but drowns later."

Fresh tears cloud Mrs. Macadem's already swollen eyes. "W-was she raped."

"No."

"Does that judge my brother works for have anything to do with it?" Mr. Macadem asks.

"We're looking at all angles. As soon as we know definitive information, I will deliver it to you. You mustn't watch the news or read the papers. We haven't made an official statement yet. Listening to people theorize will only confuse and frustrate you. Don't do that. What you hear from my mouth are the facts. This is an active investigation. Think of it as a puzzle. There are numerous parts and pieces that we have to move around. If we slide something into place before it's ready, it won't click. It will only set us back. So, while I can give you some of those puzzle pieces, I can't give you all of them until they're ready. Does that make sense?"

In unison, they nod.

I ask, "Mr. Macadem, how long have you worked at the brewery?"

"Ten years."

"Do you know the owner, Mr. Alexander?"

"Not really. He walks the floor once a week, but he doesn't talk to anyone except the supervisors."

Shifting forward in her chair, Mrs. Macadem says, "The rock quarry is part of the brewery property. Is that why you're asking that question?"

"Partly, yes." I look between them. "Did you ever hear Scarlett mention the name, Bennett Alexander?"

Mr. Macadem frowns. "As in the son of my boss? No. Scarlett wouldn't know him. He goes to that fancy academy, Fairview. Plus, he's a high schooler. Scarlett's friends are—" He pauses. "*Were* all her age."

"Did Scarlett get in trouble for anything like alcohol, cigarettes, not meeting curfew, sneaking out...anything?"

"I told you before, she's a good girl. Ask anyone." Mr. Macadem leans forward. "Are you trying to turn this around on her? Are you trying to insinuate she brought this on herself?"

"No, remember the puzzle? The only thing I'm trying to do is sort through the pieces."

Mrs. Macadem places her hand on her husband's arm. "Getting upset doesn't help anyone."

With a deep breath, he sits back in his chair.

"What is Scarlett's relationship with her Uncle Gerald?" I ask next.

Mr. Macadem grinds the palms of his hands into his eyes. "Really? Now you're asking about my brother? He was gone all weekend. Anybody could've taken that car." Shoving back from the table, he stands, looking angrily down at me. "My daughter spent her last hours terrified. Until you're ready to tell us justice has been delivered, get out of my house."

I could press, but I opt to leave.

Outside I stop at the truck where Gerald still stands. "What is the age difference between you and Jack?"

"Four years. I'm thirty-three. He's thirty-seven."

"Did you grow up in this area?"

"Yes."

"Do you know anything about The Quiet Game?"

He doesn't answer me. So much time goes by, I'm not sure he heard my question. Finally, he looks toward his brother's house. "I didn't realize that was still around."

"How do you know of it?" I ask.

"My brother created it."

EIGHTEEN

Tuesday, 4:15 p.m.

AS I'M DRIVING from the Macadem home, a text comes in from Vaughn.

Vaughn: Elle Psaltis and her mother are on their way in.
Me: Bennett?
Vaughn: Same but with father and lawyer.
Me: On my way.

I select Grace's name and send a voice text.

Me: Just checking in.
Grace: All good here. No worries.
Me: Thank you for being a great friend.
Grace: Ditto.

Fifteen minutes later, I walk into the station. Vaughn

has put Elle Psaltis and her mother in a private room. As I stride down the hall, I watch them through open blinds. With straight black hair and heavy, Mrs. Psaltis looks like an older version of Elle. They sit silently beside each other on one side of a rectangular table. Both have their arms folded over their chests and are looking at their laps.

Vaughn approaches me, carrying a laptop and the carnival photo. "They just got here. Ready?"

I follow him in, noting mother and daughter simultaneously jump when we open the door. I sit across from them. Vaughn remains standing.

Mrs. Psaltis peers at me through anxious dark brown eyes. "W-why did you want to talk with Elle?"

Vaughn hands me the carnival photo. I place it in front of the girl. With her head still down, only her eyes come up to look at it.

"This was taken Sunday at the carnival." I tap the photo. "Where did the three of you go?"

She swallows. "Nowhere. We just drove around."

I open the laptop, already feeling sick at what I'm about to do. I hate that this girl ended up in that room.

Launching the video, I turn it for them to see.

Wide-eyed and speechless, Mrs. Psaltis watches it all the way through. Elle does not. When she realizes what it is, her eyes squeeze tight.

When the video completes, I point to the time stamp. "This was filmed one hour after the carnival photo was taken. Where did Scarlett go within that hour?"

"Oh my God," Mrs. Psaltis whispers. She presses her fingers to her forehead, looking over at Elle. "What have you done?"

Elle's eyes snap open, focusing on her mother. "Nothing!" She looks at me. "We dropped Scarlett at the courthouse. That's where she wanted to go. Then me and Bennett—ya know—did that."

"Oh my God," Mrs. Psaltis whispers again. "How old is that boy?"

"Bennett Alexander is sixteen," I answer the mom, not taking my gaze off Elle. "Why did he want you to be quiet?"

"It's just a stupid game," she mumbles. "I didn't care about that."

"What did you care about?"

"That it was Bennett." Her arms tighten even more. "All the girls around town think he's cute. I wanted to be the one he likes."

"How did you two come to get in his vehicle?" I ask.

"He was at the carnival. He started flirting with Scarlett. He wanted her to go party with him. Scarlett didn't want to. I told him I would. Then Scarlett insisted she go too. We both went with him, but I didn't want her there. I wanted to be alone with him. We got into a big argument in his car. Scarlett told us just to drop her downtown at the courthouse. So, we did."

"That was the last time you saw or spoke with her?"

Elle nods.

"Why the courthouse?"

"Because that's where she disappears."

"What do you mean by 'disappears'?"

Elle's arms loosen just a bit. "We go there on Fridays for our government class. We get high school credit for it. She sneaks out. I don't know where she goes, but she always returns in time to catch the bus back to school. We're best friends. We're not supposed to have secrets. But she had that one. Yet, I always covered for her. I guess I figured she was meeting up with a boy. I thought I'd see her at school on Monday and we'd talk about our new boyfriends."

"Bennett Alexander is *not* your boyfriend!" Mrs. Psaltis explodes. She looks at me, the shock has worn out, to be replaced by anger. She waves her hand at the laptop. "You can't just let that happen. Are all those tick marks really—" her voice cuts off.

"Yes, and we're launching a separate investigation into that. Our priority right now is solving Scarlett Macadem's death." I look directly at Elle, feeling compassion for this mixed-up girl, but also irritation. She needs to know actions have consequences. "Your lies have wasted valuable time. Do you understand that?"

"I'm sorry," she mumbles.

The door opens. A woman in uniform hands Vaughn a note. He reads it before showing it to me: *The Alexanders are here.*

———

THIS TIME VAUGHN takes lead and I stand by the wall, watching. Where the Psaltises were shrunk in on themselves, the Alexanders occupy the room with a cocky air.

Vaughn shows Bennett the carnival photo. "This puts Scarlett in your vehicle the day she disappeared."

The boy gives the photo a brief, indifferent glance. "Which one's Scarlett? The fat one or the pretty one?"

He knows exactly which one Scarlett is.

Vaughn doesn't miss a beat. He points to each girl. "Elle Psaltis. Scarlett Macadem." He opens the laptop. "This one is Elle, in case you need another reminder." He presses play.

The video runs, but I don't watch it. I study Bennett whose arrogance gradually transitions into embarrassment, oddly enough. The video ends. The room falls silent. Mr. Alexander clears his throat.

"What, you can't get a girl your own age?" Vaughn asks.

"Don't say a word," the lawyer instructs.

Vaughn leaves the last image on the screen—the one of Bennett scowling into the camera while behind him Elle marks the wall with her blood. "When was the last time you saw Scarlett Macadem?"

"We dropped her at the courthouse." He looks at his father. "I swear."

"Will you close that?" Mr. Alexander nods to the laptop.

"No," Vaughn simply says, staring at Bennett. "Tell me about The Quiet Game."

The boy blinks, shocked I think that we know the term. "It's—"

"No," the lawyer interrupts. "Don't say a word. Do you have any other questions about Scarlett Macadem?"

"When you dropped her at the courthouse, where did she go?" my partner asks.

Bennett shrugs. "She walked toward Depot Hill."

NINETEEN

Tuesday, 7:15 p.m.

"AS MUCH AS I wish I could dive into Depot Hill and The Quiet Game, I've got a little brother I'm responsible for." I check the time on my phone. "I've got to go. I'll see you tomorrow morning."

Vaughn unlocks the driver's side of his Mini Cooper. "Given I have no life, I'll check out Depot Hill, which is...?"

"Public housing a few blocks from the historical downtown area. Call me if you find anything?"

"For sure."

DURING THE BRIEF drive to get my brother, the sun hovers along the surrounding Smoky Mountains, wanting to set but clinging for a few more minutes.

Matthew, Grace's husband, sits on the front porch steps watching their five-year-old run around blowing bubbles.

A big, sturdy farm boy with values rooted in family, I've always liked Matthew. He and Grace met in ninth grade and have been inseparable ever since.

"There's my favorite detective." Matthew smiles. "Go on in. Grace is in the kitchen cleaning up from dinner."

I elbow his shoulder as I pass by.

In the house the scent of grilled meat greets me. My stomach growls. The last thing I ate was the PowerBar hours ago.

Tyler lies on the couch with the three-year-old squished in beside him. A picture book sits propped open on his stomach as he reads. The little one doesn't even notice me when I lean down to press a kiss on Tyler's head. My brother spares me a brief smile, flips a page, and keeps reading.

"They are beyond cute," I say, stepping into the kitchen.

Wearing a white apron and with her red hair in its usual French braid, Grace smiles. "He is so good with my kids."

"Where's the baby?"

"Sleeping." Grace opens the oven. "Hungry?"

"For sure."

She brings out a sturdy stone plate heaped with grilled chicken, roasted asparagus, and sweet potato. My mouth waters. She puts it on the round kitchen table, and I dig in.

"Mustard?" I ask around a bite of sweet potato.

She sighs. "Well, thanks for at least trying it before requesting your disgusting condiment."

I smile.

From the refrigerator, she grabs the plain yellow and hands it to me. I squeeze it over the chicken only.

Grace pours me a glass of iced tea. "How long is he suspended for?"

"The week. Is that okay?"

"Tomorrow and Thursday I'm good, but Friday is out. Sorry. Maybe my mom?"

"Maybe." I cut off a bite of mustard chicken. "I'll figure it out."

While she finishes loading the dishwasher, I plow my way through the sweet potato.

"You got busted for pot when you were fourteen." She glances over her shoulder at me. "Remember?"

"Yes, of course, I remember."

Grace laughs. "My mom used it as a teachable moment. 'You don't want to be like Nell. Look at her sneaking around and causing her poor mom problems.'"

"She did not say that."

"She did!"

"Well, I'd like to think I've redeemed myself in Olivia's eyes."

"Of course, you have." Grace closes the dishwasher, picks up a spray bottle, and squirts the counters and stove. She begins wiping the area.

I move on to finishing the grilled chicken. "When you were in high school, did you ever hear of The Quiet Game?"

"What do you mean, like a board game?"

"More like a secret game local kids play for points. There's probably a dare involved." Grace grew up in this area, sure, but she's always been more of a Home Economics/4-H type of girl.

I would have been the one to play a daredevil game.

"No clue," she says, as expected. "Want me to ask Matthew?"

"No, all good." Leaving my asparagus right where it is, I walk my plate over to the garbage.

"Nell Brach." Grace plants both hands on her hips.

"What kind of example are you setting leaving the vegetables on your plate?"

I dump said vegetables in the garbage and slide my plate into the dishwasher. "Next time make broccoli. I hate asparagus."

"It doesn't matter that it makes your pee stink," she says. "It's good for you."

"It's also good for the garbage." I hug her. "See you in the morning with my little criminal."

A few minutes into our drive home, I tell Tyler, "You're probably going to be with Olivia on Friday."

"No," he groans. "She'll make me clean her baseboards or something."

"Well, kid, you get suspended from school and I only have so many options." In the dark car, I glance over at him. My heart pinches. The older he gets, the more he looks like our father—what I remember of him, at least. "Listen, we need to talk about punishment. I already grounded you from your phone. You have two other options. One: car wash for charity. Two: volunteer at a nursing home. Which is it going to be?"

"No option three?"

"No."

"I'll do the nursing home," he says as I figured he would. My little brother loves three things: his phone, kids, and elderly people. It won't surprise me if he one day becomes an elementary teacher or a caregiver. Given this, I guess the nursing home gig isn't really a punishment.

Oh well.

We're silent the rest of the way home. When I pull into our postage-sized house, my lights flash across someone sitting on our front steps.

I open my door and step out. The person stands.

"Hi," she says.

"Mom?"

————

DURING THE FIRST few years that Mom was incarcerated, we visited her as often as possible. Tyler would make gifts for her—pictures, Play-Doh figurines, hand-woven jewelry, and whatever else. He looked forward to our visits.

Somewhere around nine years old, he began pretending he was sick on the scheduled visitation days. By the age of ten, he stopped going altogether. I could've made him, but I didn't. Mostly because I didn't want to put Mom through his mood. She deserved better than a grouchy tween.

I never stayed home, though. No matter how busy I was, I always made time for her. It was the absolute least I could do for the sacrifice she made.

Now, I hug her hard, feeling the frail bones of her back through her sweatshirt. She's so thin. "What are you doing out?"

"I am just as confused as you. I went before a panel today, was deemed no longer a threat to society, and released."

"Why didn't you call me? How did you get home?"

"I heard about your new case. I didn't want to bother you. Holden gave me a ride."

Holden being Sheriff Owens. He visited her as much if not more than I did. They've developed a solid friendship over the years.

Smiling, she turns toward Tyler. "Hi, Sweetheart."

"Hi." He steps forward, quickly hugs her, then steps back. He takes our house key from his front jeans pocket and unlocks the door, then walks inside, leaving us on the front steps.

"I'm sorry," I whisper.

She forces a smile. "He'll come around."

TWENTY

Wednesday, 8:45 a.m.

THE MORNING ROLLS in on a thunderstorm. I leave Mom to get settled at the house, drop Tyler at Grace's, then meet Vaughn at the station.

After draping my rain jacket on my desk chair, I find my partner in the break room smearing peanut butter on an apple wedge. Today he wears a Jumanji green floral tie.

"You didn't call me last night," I say. "Does that mean Depot Hill was a flop?" I pour coffee into a mug labeled THIS IS WHAT A BADASS DETECTIVE LOOKS LIKE. From the refrigerator, I grab my coconut milk and pour some in.

After a bite of the apple, Vaughn says, "I was here when the sheriff left to go get your mom. I figured you'd be busy with that. I did go to Depot Hill. There's a community center. I found a bunch of people doing various things—homework, crafts, playing cards, etcetera. I showed Scarlett's photo around and a few people did recognize her. Said she comes by on Friday afternoons to volunteer around the center."

He puts his apple wedge down before sliding his phone from his belt clip. "As I was leaving, I walked past a wall of framed photos. They were mostly of the residents doing fun things. But this one caught my eye." He swipes his screen, taps, and hands me his phone.

I zoom in. It's a photo of several kids ranging in age from elementary to high school. With their arms slung around each other, they're all laughing and wet, like they just had a water fight. I easily locate Scarlett in the photo. But it's the man behind her that catches my eye. Smiling and soaked, he has one arm around Scarlett with the other cradling a water gun.

It's Mr. Alexander, Bennett's father.

There's a knock on the break room door. A cop just out of the academy says, "The Macadems are here to claim Scarlett's body."

IN THE SAME room where I questioned Elle Psaltis, Mr. and Mrs. Macadem sit beside each other. Situated in chairs a couple of inches apart, they keep to themselves.

With a folder and a small evidence bag, I sit down across from them. I place the bag in my lap out of sight. Opening the folder, I slide out several papers. "All you need to do is sign the bottom of each and we can release Scarlett to you. The coroner will assist in coordinating transportation if you know what funeral home." I place a pen on top.

Quietly, Mr. Macadem signs the papers before giving them to his wife. "I'm sorry." He clears his throat. "I shouldn't have told you to get out of my house. I know you're just doing your job."

I nod, accepting. "It's okay. I understand what you're going through—the anger, the frustration, the devastation... I understand. I do."

"You're the woman with the brother who went missing," Mrs. Macadem says, her voice raspy and raw.

"I am."

"So, you really do understand." Mrs. Macadem signs the last document and passes them back to me.

After placing them inside the folder, I look at her husband. "I'd like to ask you about The Quiet Game."

Mrs. Macadem visibly tenses.

"My brother mentioned you brought it up." He glances over to his wife who keeps her gaze fastened on the table between us. The muscles in her jaw flex. She's upset.

He says, "I was a mean kid back in high school. I'm not proud of my behavior. It was back when *Jackass* first came out. Do you remember that show?"

"I do," I say.

"I had a lamebrain idea to do *Jackass*-style stunts. Soon my friends were joining in. It became a competition that turned into more of a hazing. We'd get freshmen to do insane stuff and garner points. The quieter they were, the more points were awarded. It was things like jumping off bridges into water, walking on hot coals, running naked on the coldest day of the year, electrocuting yourself, and various other idiotic things. My brother carried on the 'legacy' if that's what you want to call it. I figured the whole thing petered out years after we left that place."

"Did it bleed over to Fairview Academy?" I ask.

"Yes. That was part of the competition. It was our local high school against the academy's rich kids."

"*I knew it*," Mrs. Macadem snaps, glaring at her husband. "This is your fault. Our daughter was playing that horrible game." She looks at me. "Wasn't she?"

"I don't know, but remember the puzzle pieces. This is me fiddling with one trying to see if it fits. Was there ever a sexual part to the game?"

Mrs. Macadem gasps. Her husband's eyes snap wide. "No!" he shouts. "Why would you ask that?"

"I-I thought you said she wasn't raped," Mrs. Macadem whispers.

"She wasn't." I hold up a hand. "Again, puzzle pieces. Let's move on." From my lap, I grab the small evidence bag and place it on the tabletop. Inside is a Ziploc full of small, fuzzy pink pom-poms. "We found these in Scarlett's backpack. Do they hold significance?"

Together they study them. Simultaneously, they say, "No."

I take the Ziploc back. "Did Scarlett volunteer anywhere, either recently or in the past?"

"The hospital," Mrs. Macadem answers. "She got community service hours for it. It's part of the school. Eighth graders are required to do thirty hours."

"Just the hospital?" I look between them. "Anywhere else?"

"No, nowhere else."

"What about her phone? Where is that?"

"She didn't have one." Mrs. Macadem's voice cracks. "We were getting her one for her eighth grade graduation."

A graduation she will never see.

TWENTY-ONE

Wednesday, 11 a.m.

WHAT STARTED AS A SMALL, local microbrewery rapidly grew into a nationally distributed product. White Quail Brewery is our leading employer in the area.

After parking in a visitor slot, Vaughn and I trot through the rain and into the main building that houses the gift shop, the tour office, and the executive suite.

Done in a rustic southern theme complete with mason jar lights, a mounted deer head, and reclaimed wood furniture, Mr. Alexander's office feels more like a mountain lodge than a workplace.

A sixty-something woman sits at an L-shaped desk. In the back corner, a scrap metal door leads into Mr. Alexander's area.

The secretary smiles kindly as we walk in. "Hi, can I help you?"

Vaughn shows his badge. "We'd like to speak with Mr. Alexan—"

The corner door bangs open. A brunette in her early twenties storms out. With augmented breasts, collagen lips, and a designer black and white tracksuit, she barely glances at us as she strides past. Perfume trails her wake.

Under her breath, the secretary snorts. "Don't mind her. That's his fifth mid-life crisis." She looks at her wrist that doesn't have a watch. "It's about time for her to be on the way out, cash in on alimony, and mid-life crisis number six ushered in." She stands. "I'll let him know you're here." She walks off.

Vaughn looks at me. "Interesting."

Mr. Alexander appears in the doorway. "Detectives, did I know you were coming?"

"No." I cross over, bringing up the photo of him at Depot Hill. I show it to him. "We can speak here or at the station."

WITH MR. ALEXANDER'S door closed and the secretary back out at her desk, my partner and I sit beside each other on a rich brown leather loveseat. Dressed in tan trousers with a denim shirt, Mr. Alexander occupies a matching lounge chair. Between us, a copper coffee table holds a reclaimed wood bowl with decorative balls made of twine.

In his early sixties, Ian Alexander is of average height with gray hair and a lean body that says he eats well and works out. He carries himself with confidence and authority, but not the cockiness we saw in his son, Bennett.

Once again, I bring up the photo from Depot Hill. "Why did you not mention that you knew Scarlett Macadem?"

"You didn't ask."

"We're asking you now," Vaughn replies.

"She's a good girl." He crosses his right leg over his left. "She's smart. Sweet. Shy. She has goals. She—"

"*Was* smart. Sweet. Shy. *Had* goals," I remind him.

"*Was*." He doesn't hesitate. "Of course. I've known her since the beginning of the school year. She wandered into Depot Hill one Friday afternoon. I'm on the board there and have donated from the beginning, both money and time. I spend every Friday afternoon there, some weekend days too. That Friday, we were painting one of the interior walls that had graffiti on it. She was so shy, but she finally jumped in and helped. I immediately recognized that certain something in her. It took a while to pull her from her shell, but she gradually began opening up to me. She was a small-town girl with big dreams, but not sure how to make them come true. The more I got to know her, the more I wanted those dreams to become reality. So many kids around here miss opportunities to break the cycle."

"Cycle of what?" Vaughn asks.

"Married at eighteen. Two kids by twenty-one. Never going to college or seeing the world. Working a minimum wage job. Barely making ends meet."

I think of Grace. That is her life, but one she most definitely wants to be living. "Maybe Scarlett would've been okay with that."

"No. She talked about traveling, seeing interesting places, and painting." He chuckles. "She wanted to sketch a camel. She wanted to ride that camel. She wanted to see a pyramid. And a geyser. Sail an ocean. Climb a mountain. But her parents shut her down. They wanted her to stay right here in White Quail."

"Did she tell you that?" Vaughn asks.

"Yes, we were friends. She told me things."

"Do you normally maintain friendships with thirteen-year-old girls?" I ask.

Again, he doesn't hesitate. "I was her mentor."

"Where were you on Sunday?" Vaughn asks.

"I spent Sunday afternoon at Depot Hill. I did see Scarlett. She was still there when I left to go home to my wife."

"A teenage girl was found dead this weekend in the woods next to the rock quarry, both properties you own. Additionally, you are one of the last people to see her alive." My eyes narrow. "You didn't think it was important to tell us that?"

A cunning smile curves his lips. "You didn't ask."

TWENTY-TWO

Wednesday, noon

AT 9,000 SQUARE feet with five bedrooms, seven baths, two kitchens, an infinity pool, and a guest cottage larger than the homes on my street, the Alexander estate sits on 2.63 acres overlooking a lake.

As I park, Vaughn's phone rings. He checks the number, and with an annoyed breath, says, "Give me just a second."

I wait for him on the wraparound porch. I try to give him privacy, but after several long seconds, I look at him. His head is down as he presses the phone to his ear. He's not talking, but whoever is on the other end is delivering stressful news.

He hangs up. I expect him to take a moment, but he opens the door and runs through the rain to join me.

"Everything okay?" I ask.

"Yep." He nods to the door. "I'm ready."

I ring the bell. Loudly, it gongs. Several long seconds go

by. Surprisingly, Mrs. Alexander answers. I expected a housekeeper.

We flash our badges and introduce ourselves.

Still dressed in the expensive black and white tracksuit, she moves aside and waves us in. "Didn't I see you in Ian's office a bit ago?" Her voice holds the twang that signifies she's from these parts.

"You did." I step into the foyer.

A curved stairwell leads up to the next floor. The soaring ceiling ends with a skylight dotted with rain. One long wall of glass looks out over the infinity pool and lake.

She leads us through an archway and into a feminine-decorated sitting room with mint-colored chairs, delicate white iron tables, and silk floral arrangements. Through an open door, I see a home office decorated just like Mr. Alexander's brewery suite.

"I've got Pilates in thirty minutes. Will this take long?" She sits, motioning us to do the same.

"It'll take as long as it needs," Vaughn says.

Her lips curve into a forced-patient smile. "How can I help you?"

"A thirteen-year-old girl died on Sunday. Scarlett Macadem. Do you know her?" On my phone, I pull up the photo from Depot Hill showing this woman's husband with the kids. I point to Scarlett.

"Was that taken at Depot Hill?" she asks.

"Yes. Do you know the girl?"

"No. I mean, yes, I saw the news but I don't know her."

I take my phone back. "How old are you?"

"Twenty-two."

"How long have you and Mr. Alexander been married?"

"Four years."

"Where did you meet?"

"Depot Hill. I used to live there."

Interesting. "I thought I recognized a local tone to your accent." I smile.

Her forced one stays in place. She doesn't like that her accent is local.

Vaughn says, "While Scarlett Macadem didn't live there, she used to volunteer there."

"Doesn't surprise me." She folds her arms. "She's his type."

"How's that?" I ask.

"Dark hair, blue eyes, cute, probably shy. That used to be me. I was around that age when I met Ian. He was a father figure to me. He encouraged me. He spent a lot of time helping me study. I didn't have a dad. I latched on quickly. But the more years that went by, the more our relationship changed. Soon it wasn't about me going off to college, it was me waiting to turn eighteen so that I could marry him and start a family. He made promises. I believed them. He divorced wife number four and we got married on my birthday." Shaking her head, she looks away. "Let's just say my life hasn't turned out how I thought."

On a glass-topped table beside her, a phone lights up. She gives it a cursory glance before turning it with the face down.

"Do you mind getting me some water?" Vaughn asks.

With a nod, she leaves the sitting area. My partner and I move in sync. I reach for her phone as Vaughn strides into the attached home office. Her cell is password protected, but I easily swipe the home screen noting multiple missed calls from Ian Alexander all placed in the time it took us to drive from the brewery to here.

Vaughn emerges from the home office right as Mrs.

Alexander returns with bottled water. She pauses when she notes we're both standing.

"One last question," Vaughn says. "Where were you on Sunday?"

"With my mom at a spa in Gatlinburg."

I take the water bottle from her. "We're going to need your mom's name."

———

FROM THE ALEXANDER MANSION, we go straight back to the brewery. Luckily, Mr. Alexander is in the parking lot climbing into a white Mercedes.

I don't bother with niceties. I pull up right beside him and roll my window down. "You lied to us."

Standing under an umbrella, he looks at me.

"You weren't home with your wife on Sunday. Turns out she was on a mother-daughter spa trip in Gatlinburg."

"Any further questions are to be addressed to my lawyer. You have his contact." With that, he climbs into the driver's side and backs out.

"He's officially a pain in my ass."

TWENTY-THREE

Wednesday, 1:30 p.m.

WE MAKE a quick stop at Starbucks, each grabbing a beverage and a protein box. Save for one customer sitting with headphones and a laptop, the place is empty. We choose a table in the far corner.

"So, Ian Alexander lied." Vaughn takes the lid off of his hot green tea.

"That he did. Also, when I looked at the wife's phone, I noted that he placed eleven calls to her in the time it took us to drive from the brewery to his home."

"Needing an alibi?"

"Perhaps."

As we eat, Vaughn begins exploring hypothetical scenarios of this past weekend. "On Sunday, Elle drops Scarlett off at the courthouse. Scarlett then walks to Depot Hill. Ian Alexander was there, but he didn't leave alone as he said. Scarlett went with him. Mrs. Alexander was on her mother-daughter trip, so he had the mansion all to himself. Scarlett's parents had already given her permission to be gone the night. Mr. Alexander knows this. He plans things: pizza, a movie, staying over in the guest suite, and other non-threatening things. On Sunday night they go for a drive and end up at the quarry. He makes a move on her. She doesn't like it. There's a struggle..." Vaughn eyes the hard-boiled egg I just dipped in mustard. "Are you seriously going to eat that?"

As a response, I do.

"You weren't kidding."

"Try it."

He does, dipping his egg into my mustard and eating. "Okay, not so bad."

I move on to doing the same thing with my cheese. "Back to Scarlett: then how did she end up in a car belonging to the judge?"

My partner wipes his hands on his jeans before pulling up a photo on his phone. "I took this while I was in Alexander's home office." It's a picture of Ian and Ronan Aaron dressed in hunting gear, posing behind a deer. "Did they do it together?"

Nausea bitters my mouth.

Vaughn puts his phone away. "Maybe this has nothing to do with that stupid game. Maybe this is about Mr. Alexander prowling for future wife number six. When he realizes Scarlett isn't cooperating, he calls his buddy Judge Aaron. They stuff her in the back and push the car into the quarry. They never expected her to claw her way free. If the car is found, fingers will point to Gerald Macadem, as he's the driver of the vehicle."

"Lot of holes there." I sip my coffee. "Like why not bury her? Why put her in a car?"

"And why not the trunk? Why the backseat?"

My thoughts shift with those puzzle pieces. Silently, we eat.

On my phone, I pull up the crime scene photos. I look first at the gray sneaker left in the back. Then I study the frantic claw marks as she tried to open the door. Next, I look at the bruising on her ribs from climbing through the window, fighting her way to the surface and much-needed air. Other than normal bruising and scraping, she hadn't been touched.

"Do you have the tox screen?" I ask.

Vaughn sifts through his phone, finding the file. "No opiates, amphetamines, marijuana, alcohol, or barbiturates. What are you thinking?"

"Anesthetics. There's hardly any bruising on her body. She was unconscious. She didn't come to until she was under the water. Whoever put her in the back thought she was already—"

"Dead."

From my protein box, I eat a cheese wedge. "I would put the body in the trunk, though... Why the backseat?"

"Sloppy work? In a hurry? Didn't know how to open the trunk?"

"Let's get a test for anesthetics added to the samples."

While my partner places a call to the lab, I look at the photo of Scarlett's postmortem glassy eyes.

"Nell?"

I glance up, seeing my mom hovering just inside the coffee shop. In an old patterned dress she wore once upon a time, she hesitantly looks between me and Vaughn. For seven years now I've seen her in a variety of white sweats and tees surrounded by others dressed the same—either in the family visitation room or the courtyard on pretty days. It's the oddest thing seeing her here, out in public.

Through the glass door behind her, I spy Grandpa's old Chevy truck, the ever-present dirt on it streaked from the rain.

"Mom." I wave her over.

With her light brown hair smoothed back in a ponytail, she approaches. She wears mascara and peach-tinted lip gloss. "You look pretty." Standing, I hug her. "What are you doing here?"

"Applying for a job. As part of my release, I need one."

I motion for her to sit.

Vaughn hangs up his call. He gets up, pulling out a chair for my mom. I love that he just did that. I make the introductions.

"It's very nice to meet you, Ms. Brach." He smiles kindly.

"Call me Jill." She places her beat-up white purse in her lap. "I didn't mean to interrupt."

"It's fine. We're just finishing up." I offer her the almonds in my protein box. I know how much she loves them.

She eats one. "You could've left Tyler with me today."

"Oh...that's okay. Grace had already agreed."

"Tomorrow then?"

"Maybe." Tyler would rather pick up garbage along the side of the highway than stay with Mom. I have a lot to figure out with the two of them.

"I was thinking of grounding him." Delicately, she clears her throat. "But I wanted to check with you first. I wasn't sure how you handle his punishments."

"Oh, um, I already took care of that."

A flush crawls into her cheeks. "Of course, you did. I-I don't know what I was thinking."

Inside, I wince. I want her to feel at home and comfortable, not on edge. Lightly, I grasp her lower arm. "We'll figure all this out. It's more important to get you settled in, don't you think? We'll get our routine down. I promise."

With a nod, she stands. "Guess I better go get this application filled out." She presses a kiss on the top of my head. "I love you."

"Love you too."

She turns to Vaughn. "Nice to meet you."

"Likewise, Jill."

After she walks off, I turn back to my partner. Awkwardness fills the air between us. Or perhaps it's more on my end because he seems fine as he busies himself taking our items to the garbage, then going to the restroom.

The thing is, I've had custody of Tyler since he was six and Mom went away. I have been the parent. Things like punishments are not what Mom and I talk about when we see each other. I'm thrown for a bit of a loop here. I didn't think she would come back and expect to step right back into the mom role.

I know she wants to reconnect with my little brother. She wants to be involved and for me to know I'm not alone. I get it. I just don't know what my life is supposed to look like now. Even before she went away, I played a huge part in parenting Tyler. Hell, I played a huge part in parenting Mom.

Over the years she's been incarcerated I've developed a respect for her that I never had before. I will figure this out. For me, sure, but mostly for Mom and Tyler.

As I wait on Vaughn, I bring up the photo I was looking at before my mom came over.

Scarlett's lifeless eyes stare back.

"What did you see before you died?" I whisper.

IN THE CAR, the phone rings. It's Sheriff Owens. "Well, you two are causing quite the problem," he says, his tone amused.

"Oh?" I share a smile with my partner.

"Ian Alexander's lawyer called me. He thought it was *very* unprofessional that you went to his client's office without an appointment, not once, but twice. He reminded me just exactly who Mr. Alexander is—our county's leading employer, an active member of the community, and a huge donor to my next sheriff's campaign. Any further questions are to be directed to him and a meeting is to be put on the calendar. His words, not mine."

"Noted," I say. "He saw Scarlett on Sunday at Depot Hill. According to him, he left and went home to his wife. We caught him in a lie. His wife was gone on a mother-daughter trip. We're heading to Depot Hill to question the residents. If we find an eyewitness that puts Scarlett leaving with him, we'll bring him in."

"Have you talked to the mother?" Sheriff Owens asks.

"That's on our list as well. Don't worry we will cross every t and dot every i. We're both aware of how influential Ian Alexander is." Flicking on my blinker, I merge onto the county road that leads into downtown White Quail. "Do you know when the funeral is?"

"Tomorrow morning. It's graveside, family only." In the background, I hear a woman telling the sheriff he has another call.

We say goodbye.

Vaughn's been looking at his phone this whole time. He glances up. "Guess where Mrs. Alexander's mother still lives?"

Depot Hill. "Perfect. How about I take her and you start questioning the residents?"

TWENTY-FOUR

Wednesday, 2:45 p.m.

IN A SMALL AND cleanly decorated one-bedroom apartment, I sit across from Yvonne Hardy, Mrs. Alexander's mother. With permed brown hair and acne-scarred tan skin, she looks nothing like her trophy wife of a daughter.

After showing Ms. Hardy my badge and introducing myself, I say, "We're talking to as many residents as we can about Scarlett Macadem. Do you know who that is?"

"Yes, that's the little girl who was found dead over the weekend."

"She used to volunteer here in the community room. Did you ever see her?"

"Sure, time and again. We never really interacted though. Ian—*Mr. Alexander*—always kept her busy."

"What do you mean?"

"Oh, with the kids he has his favorites."

"Was your daughter once one of his 'favorites?'"

Yvonne's pleasant smile falters. "Yes, Mary-Anne certainly was. He's got a thing for young brunettes."

"How long have you lived here?"

"Since I was sixteen. I got pregnant with Mary-Anne. My boyfriend wanted nothing to do with me. My daddy kicked me out. The state paid for me to stay here at Depot Hill in the teen group home. Eventually, I aged out and moved into this little one-bedroom. Been here ever since. Raised Mary-Anne here."

"What do you do for a living?"

"I have a couple of part-time jobs." She glances at her phone. "One of which I've got to get to in thirty minutes."

"I would think with who your daughter is married to that you would've had the opportunity to move out of here."

Yvonne huffs an unamused laugh. "No, thank you. I don't want anything from that man. I've never liked Mr. Alexander. He's a pompous ass. I told Mary-Anne she'd regret her decision to marry him. But she wouldn't listen." She shakes her head. "It's coming back now to bite her hard. Divorce isn't far off. And with the pitiful prenup she signed, she'll be right back here living with me. Watch."

"Ms. Hardy, where were you on Sunday?"

"I had a birthday. My daughter took me to Gatlinburg for a spa getaway. Or rather she dropped me, left, came back, left... She was in and out so much, my head spun."

"Where'd she go?"

"Home, I guess."

Given there are thirty miles between Gatlinburg and White Quail, it's not like it's just around the corner. "She didn't tell you?"

"No, and I've learned not to ask questions. I should be upset. It was my birthday, after all, but I'm tryin' to be understanding. Something's going on at home. Whatever it is, I think it came to a head over the weekend."

"What time on Sunday did you last see her?"

"I fell asleep around nine. She was in our room then, and she was there when I woke up in the morning."

———

IN THE HALL outside of Ms. Hardy's apartment, I run into Vaughn. He's already talking, "I found an eyewitness that puts Scarlett at five p.m. on Sunday climbing into—you ready for this—a white Mercedes."

TWENTY-FIVE

Wednesday, 6 p.m.

AFTER TRACKING DOWN THE ALEXANDERS, we bring them in and put them in separate rooms. We decide to start with Mr. Alexander.

He and his lawyer sit across the table from me. Sheriff Owens and Vaughn stand along the wall. The sheriff doesn't need to be in here. He's silently showing that he doesn't care how deep Mr. Alexander's pockets are.

I say, "Where were you Sunday afternoon?"

"I already told you. I spent some time at Depot Hill. I did see Scarlett. I left and went home to my wife."

"Was your wife there or still at the spa?"

"She arrived sometime later."

"Did you know she would be returning home?"

"No, it was a surprise."

"So, you really didn't 'go home to her.'"

Silence.

"Either way, those were details you could've told us earlier," I say.

"You didn't ask."

I knew he was going to respond like that.

"Did she stay home for the evening?" I ask.

"No, she went back to join her mother."

"What did you do after she left?"

"I did laps in my pool. Watched TV. Ate. Normal things people do on a Sunday night."

"Why so much back and forth from the spa?"

"Because we're fighting. Something couples do. Mary-Anne is trying to catch me with another woman."

"Is there another woman?"

The lawyer shifts forward. "Mr. Alexander's marriage is off the table. What questions do you have about Scarlett Macadem?"

"Do you drive a white Mercedes?"

"I do."

"We have an eyewitness that puts Scarlett Macadem getting into a white Mercedes at five p.m. on Sunday."

Mr. Alexander looks over at Sheriff Owens. "Is that what this is about? You should've done your homework, Sheriff. My wife also drives a white Mercedes."

IN MRS. ALEXANDER'S ROOM, Vaughn takes lead while I stand to the side. The sheriff isn't present for this one.

"I'll get right to things," Vaughn says. "We spoke with your mother. She said you were in and out of the spa several times on Sunday. Where did you go?"

Mrs. Alexander looks over at her lawyer. It's not the

same lawyer that her husband uses. This one is a woman. She nods her head, letting her client know she should answer.

"I think Ian's having an affair. I came back here to White Quail to spy on him. If I can catch him in the act, our prenup is void. I can divorce him and get my money. So, yes, Mama was right. I was in and out on Sunday. Ian thought I was going to be gone. I figured he let his guard down."

"And did he?"

"Not that I saw."

"Do you drive a white Mercedes?" Vaughn asks.

"Yes, and I think that's part of the problem."

"How is that?"

"It's not a car that exactly blends in. If I'm truly going to spy on him, I need a different vehicle."

"We have an eyewitness that puts Scarlett Macadem getting into a white Mercedes on Sunday at five in the afternoon."

Mrs. Alexander sighs. "That was me."

"Earlier today when we came to your home, you said you didn't know the girl."

"I didn't, not really. Plus, what was I supposed to say? I gave a dead girl a ride?"

"Yes, that is exactly what you should have said."

"Listen, I was sitting outside Depot Hill. Ian was there. I saw him leave. I was about to follow when this cute girl walked toward my car. She waved. I rolled my window down. She stopped. I think she thought I was Ian. 'What do you want?' I snapped. She was so startled that her eyes welled up with tears. I felt horrible. After I got her calmed down, I asked who she was. When I heard her last name was Macadem, I figured she was probably related to Gerald. There's no other Macadems around here that I know of.

Anyway, I offered her a ride. She got in. I took her to her uncle's place. He's a live-in nanny for Judge Aaron. From there I went home to find Ian alone swimming in our pool. We argued. I went back to join Mama at the spa. And that is where I stayed until Monday morning."

"How do you know Gerald Macadem?"

She blushes. "We're...friends."

TWENTY-SIX

Thursday, 8:45 a.m.

AFTER WEDNESDAY'S RAIN, Thursday dawns a perfect and sunny, crisp spring day. Despite my conversation with Mom at Starbucks, I drive Tyler to Grace's house.

"You haven't said much to Mom since she's been home," I say.

He shrugs.

I get it. Mom's basically a stranger to him. His most recent memories are buried in our visits to the mental hospital. The last year of which was a constant battle. It wore me out. I gave up making him go. I figured it was doing more harm than good.

Now I wonder.

I constantly question my ability with my brother. I never know if I'm making the right decisions or not. Maybe if I was his real mom, I'd feel more secure. Who the hell knows? He is the only aspect of my life that I *do* question. I'm such a confident person otherwise.

"How about I plan an outing this weekend?" I suggest. "Just the three of us."

"Don't you have Scarlett's death to solve?"

"Yes, but I can do both."

He looks away from the road and out his side window.

"Tyler?"

He shrugs again.

I know that shrug. I invented it. It means one wall has gone up, to be followed by many more if I press. He is so much like me—strong-willed, independent, determined, not easily swayed, but he does care deeply for a select few. Where we differ is that I'm outspoken to his perpetual quietness.

What he needs is a mentor.

As much as I would love to be that, unfortunately, I'm not. That doesn't bother me as much as the fact he doesn't seem to look up to anybody. Instead, he flounders his way through each day. At least I had Grandpa who I listened to. One thing is for sure though—if he were still alive, he'd know what to say to Tyler because he always knew what to say to me.

Structure, boundaries, rules. That's what that kid needs. And there's nothing wrong with a swift swat to the butt.

That's what Grandpa would say to me. However, with Tyler's history of abandonment from our father, being abducted at six, and then seeing his mother incarcerated, I tend to handle him with cautious gloves. Maybe I do need to crack down more.

After delivering him to Grace, I drive to the other side of town where Scarlett Macadem is being laid to rest.

Quietly, I pull up under a tree and park in line with several other vehicles. I roll my window down. Across the small lawn spattered with gravestones, the Macadem family stands next to a freshly dug plot draped in artificial turf. A white and pink closed coffin sits perched on a casket-lowering system, ready to be put into the ground. Beside it, a gold-framed photo of Scarlett sits up high on an easel.

Holding a Bible, a priest softly reads. While I listen to his voice trail through the air, I study the family.

Dressed in a dark suit, Jack Macadem stands with his feet braced wide and his arms behind his back. He stares at Scarlett's coffin, his face a blank mask. One foot away, Nina Macadem is dressed in a dark skirt and tucked-in blouse. Unlike her husband, her face is a mask of devastation. One of the elementary-aged twins holds Mrs. Macadem's right hand while the other grips her left leg. Like their mother, their little faces show the overwhelming emotion that comes with losing a loved one. Two couples I'd place in their late sixties are there as well, most likely the grandparents.

Uncle Gerald hovers in the space between his brother and sister-in-law. From across the graveyard, he makes eye contact with someone parked a few spaces in front of me. Unfortunately, a large van between me and the unknown person prohibits my view.

Slowly, Scarlett is lowered into the ground. Nina begins to cry. Both grandmothers lay flowers on the casket as it disappears. When it's to the bottom, Jack steps forward, takes a handful of dirt, and sprinkles it over the open grave. The priest says a few more words, then the family turns away, leaving the groundskeepers to finish filling in the hole.

The family walks away from the line of cars where I'm parked and toward the funeral home where they're likely holding a reception. As they do, Mr. Macadem places a hand on his wife's lower back that she brushes off.

Grief either brings people together or pushes them apart. I can only hope they work through this barrier and come back together. The twins need them, and *they* need each other.

I step from my vehicle, walk past the van in front, and spy Ronan Aaron sitting in his sports car.

Through his open window, he looks up at me. "Hi."

"What are you doing here?" I don't bother hiding the irritation in my tone. "Family only."

He takes off his black-framed sunglasses and secures them in the front of his polo shirt. "I'm paying my respects, Nell. That's all. I'll go."

I wait for him to start his engine and do just that, but he doesn't. Instead, he grips the wheel and looks out the windshield.

"I'm not used to this side of you," he quietly says.

"What side is that?"

"Cold. Hard. Emotionally distant." He looks up at me again. "I don't like it."

Ronan is one of the few people who have seen the softer side of me. Though I am a detective and that does require a level of compartmentalization, I don't want to be a robot. It's important to keep emotionally available. The fact that he just said I was the opposite bothers me. Perhaps I'm over-compensating for the personal history I have with him. "I'm doing my job. A job you happen to be part of this time around."

He turns on his car. The engine rumbles low. He puts his sunglasses back on. "Be careful with Ian Alexander." With that, Judge Ronan Aaron drives off.

Back in my vehicle, a text comes in from Vaughn.

Vaughn: Heard back from the lab. She tested positive for Rohypnol. Also, get here ASAP. We have another eyewitness.

TWENTY-SEVEN

Thursday, 11:15 a.m.

WHEN I ARRIVE at the station, Vaughn is speaking to a man in his early twenties. "I heard you were asking around about the Alexanders. I didn't think anything about what happened Sunday night. My girlfriend's the one who insisted I come in."

Today Vaughn wears a pink Sasquatch tie with a powder blue button-down that the guy can't seem to stop looking at. "What happened Sunday night?" my partner asks.

"I was paddleboarding the lake. It was a full moon. The perfect time to be on the water. I like that spot of the lake that trails the fancy homes. I was coasting past the Alexander mansion and I heard arguing. I should've just kept going, but I was being nosy, I guess. They were standing in the backyard. It was hard to see because they were in the shadows. Hard to hear. But I half expected them to throw down in a fistfight. But then the taller of the two picked something up and put it over his shoulder"—the young man mimics the movement—"fireman style. It was dark, but I'm pretty sure it was a body."

"What time was this?" I ask.

"Around ten at night."

"The Alexanders are roughly the same height," Vaughn says. "What do you mean the taller of the two?"

"Oh, sorry, it wasn't a man and a woman. It was two men. Again, it was dark, but I'm pretty sure the taller one was bald."

WITH A STATEMENT down from our new eyewitness, I toast a bagel and give half to Vaughn.

"You and I both know the tall bald man is Ronan Aaron," he says.

I nod.

"He was supposedly home with his son on Sunday night."

Again, I nod.

"Want me to circle back to the judge?"

Another nod.

We're silent after that, eating, and idly watching the local news. A story on pet adoption merges into the next.

A reporter says, "Four days ago thirteen-year-old Scarlett Macadem was found dead in the woods near White Quail's rock quarry. She had previously been in a vehicle found at the bottom of the quarry belonging to Judge Ronan Aaron. Both the rock quarry and the woods are owned by Ian Alexander, president, and CEO of White Quail Brewery. Today the Macadem family laid her to rest. No arrest has been made. What you're about to see next is not for a young viewer. This is a photo of the vehicle that she escaped from."

A picture pops up of the back door with the claw marks visible and zoomed in on in. Right above it and stuck in the window's seam is a swatch of Scarlett's emerald-colored top.

"Oh, no." Vaughn looks at me. "How did they get that?"

With the amount of butter that I put on my bagel, it shouldn't be dry, but the last bite feels like sandpaper when I swallow. "I don't know."

"Sheriff Owens is going to be pissed."

"Yes, he is."

The lobby receptionist flags me down. "Jack Macadem is here."

"Head on to the courthouse," I tell Vaughn. "I'll handle Mr. Macadem."

TWENTY-EIGHT

Thursday, 11:55 a.m.

STILL DRESSED in the suit I saw him in earlier, I meet Mr. Macadem in the lobby.

"I saw you at the funeral," he says. "And Judge Aaron."

The door to the lobby opens. Two cops in uniform walk in. They disappear into the back. The door opens again. A woman and child walk in, going to the receptionist's desk.

"Why don't we go somewhere private?" I suggest.

"It was family only."

"I know that. It's why I stayed in my vehicle. I was resp—"

Mr. Macadem holds up a hand. "My girls want to know if the bad man is coming for them. What the hell am I supposed to say to that?"

The woman looks over her shoulder at us.

"Mr. Macadem, let's speak privately." I move toward the security door that opens to the back of the station.

"No. When are you going to make an arrest? When can I tell my wife justice has been served?"

"We will make an arrest as soon as we can."

"Is this the part where you explain the puzzle pieces again?" He takes one intimidating step closer. "It was the judge. Even my brother knows it. He quit his job. He doesn't want anything to do with that man."

"I one hundred percent understand your fury. I know it is clawing at you hot and insistent. You wake with it if you can even sleep. You dream of it. You dwell on it while you do daily mundane things like brush your teeth and shower. Hell, I was you seven years ago with my brother. I am the exact person to be investigating this case. I want justice just as much as you."

"I'll take things into my own hands if need be." His face hardens.

"Believe me when I say if you do that it will spiral out of control. You will regret it and it will trickle down to your whole family."

His jaw flexes. His gaze is so powerful that the muscles in my arms and neck automatically tense. Like I'm ready for a fight.

Mr. Macadem's eyes move off of me and up to the corner where a TV is mounted here in the lobby. A raspy breath scrapes in and down his throat. I turn, seeing the photo of the claw marks on the news again.

Oh shit.

"Turn that off!" I yell to the receptionist.

She scrambles to do so.

"How could you?" he whispers.

"I didn't." I hold my hands up. "I assure you I did not give anyone that photo."

His voice comes low. "If I found out you did, you are done." With that, he storms from the station.

———

IN MY VEHICLE, I scream. I punch the seat. I slam my hand into the steering wheel. This is not happening. Who the hell leaked that photo?

Across the lot, something catches my attention. I glance up, seeing my partner sitting behind the wheel of his Mini Cooper listening to someone on his phone. I thought he already left. He does not look happy.

I keep watching.

Shaking his head, he fires off a reply, then hangs up and throws his phone onto his dash. He takes his sunglasses off and presses his fingers into his eyes. He sits that way for several seconds, his shoulders lifting and falling with deep breaths.

Eventually, he puts his sunglasses on, starts his car, and drives out the other end of the lot. Whatever is going on with him is not about this case.

It's also none of my business.

However, Scarlett Macadem *is* my business.

Now that we have Mary-Anne Alexander's statement, I need to circle back to Uncle Gerald.

I dial his number. He picks up after the second ring. "Hello?"

"Detective Brach here. I just saw your brother. He said you quit your job working for Judge Aaron. Where are you currently living?"

"I temporarily moved back in with my parents. They live on Benson Drive. Why?"

"I'd like to speak with you. Is that where you are now?"

"No, I'm still at the cemetery. I told my family I'd handle wrapping up everything here. They've all gone home. Except for Jack, I guess. I didn't realize he had come to see you."

"Please stay there. I'm on my way."

TWENTY-NINE

Thursday, 12:45 p.m.

WHEN I ARRIVE BACK at the cemetery, Gerald is leaning against a red vintage Cadillac near where I had parked earlier. He took his suit jacket off and loosened his tie. The grounds people have finished. Other than a woman on the other side of the graveyard kneeling and praying, we are the only two people around.

I park behind him and get out. "Interesting choice of vehicle."

"It's my parents'."

"Did you quit your job or did Ronan Aaron fire you?"

"No, I quit. I couldn't work for a man connected to my niece's death. I have to be loyal to my brother. It bothered him I was still working there. I had a conversation with Ronan and he understood. Honestly, I think he was relieved. He wants to be removed from all of this as well."

"What is your relationship with Mary-Anne Alexander?"

"We're... friends." He clears his throat. "Why?"

"Were you aware that Mrs. Alexander dropped Scarlett off at your prior residence on Sunday at approximately five thirty in the afternoon?"

"I know now, yes. She told me she talked with you. I don't know what to tell you. Like I said, I was gone all weekend with a buddy. If she dropped Scarlett at my old place, I don't know where my niece went after that. I'm sorry. I wish I had more."

"Did Scarlett know you'd be gone?"

"No, I didn't tell her. But I have a 'Gone Fishing' sign that I hang on my apartment door. If she saw that, she knew."

"Do you know what Rohypnol is?"

His eyes widen. "Why would you ask me that?"

Interesting response. "Answer the question."

"Yes, it's the 'date rape' drug."

"Have you ever used it?"

"Why?"

"Answer the question."

"No, of course not."

"What time on Sunday did you arrive home from your 'buddy' weekend?"

"Didn't you already ask me that question?"

"Answer it again."

"Around nine o'clock? Why, am I suspect?"

"Should you be?"

"I didn't kill my niece!"

"I didn't say you did."

THIRTY

Thursday, 3 p.m.

BACK AT THE STATION, I check in with Vaughn via
text.

Me: Are you still at the courthouse?
Vaughn: Yes. Judge Aaron has been in session since I
arrived. I haven't had the chance to speak with him. I don't
think it matters though.
Me: Why?
Vaughn: You didn't hear? Our paddleboarding eyewitness
flaked. He said he was mistaken.
Me: It's been four hours. How could he have flaked in four
hours?
Vaughn: Maybe he realized what two men he saw and just
how powerful they are. I'm still going to hang around.

   In my peripheral, I see the sheriff coming from his office

with Tyler in tow. He sees me and redirects my brother toward my desk.

"What are you doing here?" I ask.

"Grace dropped me off. She said she texted you."

"Oh. I've been so busy I didn't notice." I nod for him to sit at Vaughn's desk.

"Are you texting with Detective London?" Sheriff Owens asks.

"I am, yes. I heard our eyewitness flaked?"

"That's right. If Vaughn's still at the courthouse, he needs to leave."

With a nod, I quickly text my partner what the sheriff said.

Tyler picks up a pen and spins it around his right fingers. He's tried to teach me that trick multiple times and I can never seem to make it happen. "Why can't Grace watch me tomorrow?"

"Because she's got stuff to do."

"I don't want to stay with Mom," he murmurs.

I make myself not look up at Owens. "Not here. We'll talk about that later."

"You can hang with me," the sheriff says.

Tyler stops with the pen. He looks up, stunned. "Really?" he asks, so excited his voice cracks on the last syllable.

I can't remember the last time my brother was eager about anything.

"Ride in with your sister," Owens says. "I'll take you from there."

"All right." Tyler sits up. "Awesome."

The sheriff nods to his office. "Nell, a word."

I follow him in, closing the door. The air shifts, becoming serious. He doesn't sit at his desk. He remains standing, looking at me. "This is your first lead case."

"Yes."

"I am not happy about the leaked photo. That's twice now a reporter has latched onto details before the information was released. The first one I overlooked. Any reporter with half a brain could figure out the name Ronan Aaron. But this photo is a different beast. You told me you would cross every t with this one. This one especially, Nell. What is going on? Why the sloppy work? Are you not ready to be the lead? There's no shame in admitting that. Or are you too emotionally connected given your relationship with Judge Aaron?"

"No, I am focused. I am impartial. I am ready to be the lead investigator. I *am* crossing every t." Or at least I thought I was. "I don't know how the leak occurred. We don't even have an evidence board up where anyone back here could see. Vaughn and I have everything on our phones and laptops. Someone would have to hack into our devices to gain access to that photo..." My voice trails as an unsettling thought nudges in.

Is Vaughn the leak?

No. No, of course not. The last thing I need to do is question my partner.

Sheriff Owens looks away from me and out the window that overlooks the workroom and my desk. Tyler still sits there, back to spinning the pen and staring at us.

The sheriff says, "I hate saying this, but one more mistake and you're off the case."

"That won't happen."

THIRTY-ONE

Thursday, 4:15 p.m.

ON THE DRIVE HOME, Tyler fiddles with a hangnail on his thumb. He went from lit up and excited to sullen and withdrawn.

"You're quiet," I say.

"Are you in trouble? I saw the sheriff talking to you. It didn't look good."

"It's nothing you need to worry about." I pull into our neighborhood and park. "I'm dropping you off. I still have work to do."

My brother doesn't move.

"Tyler?"

"Will you come in with me?" he mumbles. "Just for a few minutes?"

"Okay," I quietly say, already knowing I'm going to work from home for the next few hours. That's okay. It'll give me a chance to review everything and jot down notes.

In the house, Mom has cleaned from top to bottom and

everything in between. I inhale whatever it is she's got in the Crock-Pot. "Smells good." I can quickly get used to this.

"Chili." She turns away from stirring it to look at the TV in our living room. That damn photo is once again being flashed. "Why in the world did you all release that horrible picture? I can't imagine how that's affecting the family."

"We didn't." I loop my windbreaker over a wall-mounted hook and toss my keys onto a nearby console table.

Tyler disappears down the hall into his room.

In my bedroom, I place my gun in the safe, and sitting on the bed, I scroll my phone for messages.

Someone would have to hack into our devices to gain access to that photo.

I frown.

Pulling up my email, I roll through all the recently sent messages. Nothing is off. I bring up my call log next. Again, nothing seems out of place. Same with my texts. I tap on my photos, going to the folder reserved for work. I pull up the one of the claw marks and click "share." Two names pop up: Vaughn, of course, and Tyler.

I see red.

I'm off my bed and out of my room in a second. I don't knock. I throw open Tyler's door. "You little son of a bitch. Do you realize what you've done? I could've gotten fired today! Why, Tyler? Why would you do that? You have destroyed the Macadem family. You have hurt them horribly. You've quite possibly damaged the entire case."

He lies on his bed face up, staring at the ceiling. Like he was waiting on me. "I'm sorry," he murmurs.

"That's not good enough! What the hell possessed you to do that?"

"The stupid game. I was asked to play The Quiet

Game. I was supposed to find a photo, preferably of Scarlett dead, and send it to an email address. I couldn't do the dead one. So, I did the door."

Anger throbs through the veins in my neck. "Who asked you to do this?"

"I don't know," he whispers. "I got an email." He sits up, crossing his long legs and looking away from me out the window. "Let me guess, you want me to tell the sheriff."

"Hell, no, you're not telling Owens! And you're sure as shit not going with him tomorrow on some sort of field trip. You're going to stay right here with Mom while I figure out how to deal with you."

Slowly, Tyler looks over at me. His eyes narrow. The muscles in his jaw clench. I've never seen him like that. Sulky, sure. Quiet, all the time. Petulant, soft-spoken, grumpy, but never angry.

"Why don't you just send me to live with Dad?" he snaps. "Then you won't have to worry about where you're putting me or how you're dealing with me."

"Dad?" I scoff. "News flash, he hasn't been in our lives, ever. Why would you think he would be now?"

"Because we've been emailing!" he shouts.

"You've been *what*?"

"Just go!" he screams. "GET OUT OF MY ROOM."

I slam his door, and with fists clenched, I stand in the hall shaking.

When I finally look up, Mom's in the archway that leads into the kitchen. Softly, she smiles. "Come have some chili. You two need space."

I DO NOT STAY and eat chili. I leave and drive around, trying to calm down.

I don't know what to do with Tyler. How do parents deal with this shit?

Parents...

Maybe that's what it boils down to. I am not Tyler's parent. I am his legal guardian. Would being his parent give me the wisdom to deal with this? I don't know.

Has he really been exchanging emails with our father? I can't remember the last time I talked with that man. It was definitely back in Georgia before we moved here to Tennessee. Tyler was just a toddler.

How is this affecting Mom? She hasn't mentioned Dad's name in years. Which is a positive thing given how much she held the naïve hope he'd magically walk back into our lives. I figured she'd finally accepted his absence. I hope I'm right.

But now Tyler has taken on Mom's naivety.

I always thought my brother was more like me than anybody, but he does have so much of our mother in him. Somehow, I've overlooked that.

With Mom, though, I've learned her emotional frailty is a foundation for her strength.

I can learn from that.

My phone rings. I don't recognize the number. Over Bluetooth, I answer, "Detective Brach here."

"It's Ophelia."

Ronan's secretary. "Everything okay?"

"Do you have time to talk? I'll come to you."

"I'm pulling into the station now."

"See you in a few," she says, then hangs up.

THIRTY-TWO

Thursday, 5:30 p.m.

AS USUAL, Ophelia is put together from top to bottom with diamond earrings, black hair perfectly curled, a purple pantsuit, and beige heels. However, unlike every other time I've seen her, this evening her face holds no pleasantness.

She looks directly at me with worried eyes. "I waffled all day on coming here."

"Would you like something?" Vaughn gently asks. "We have herbal tea, coffee, water…"

"No, thank you. I just want to get this over with." She shoots a nervous look around the closed-in room.

Reaching across the table, I touch her hand. "Don't let this atmosphere throw you off. You came in here for a reason. Look at me and remember we're friends. Talk to me like that, okay? Forget I'm a detective."

Ophelia blows out a shaky breath that vibrates through her body. I have never seen her like this. It worries me.

Moving my chair around the table, I sit beside her and take her hand again.

"You know I've been at the courthouse forever. I pride myself on that. I know how to hear things and forget them. It's why I've worked for judges, the mayor, and other city officials. Do you know what I mean?"

"Of course."

"For the first time, though, I feel the need to say something." Her hand that grips mine turns clammy. "Yesterday Judge Aaron was on the phone with Mr. Alexander. While they weren't yelling, it was not a friendly conversation. I heard words like 'passport,' 'DNA test,' 'dealing with the situation,' and 'keeping things quiet.' I don't know, Nell. Maybe it's nothing, but given what's going on with the Macadem girl, I thought I'd better talk to you."

"You've done the right thing." I keep holding her hand. "It's going to be okay. Thank you for telling us all of this. It's what we needed."

"Also, they are meeting tonight at City Park."

THIRTY-THREE

Thursday, 8 p.m.

CITY PARK IS where I run. I'm very familiar with its trails, ponds, playgrounds, and athletic fields. We opt to take Vaughn's Mini Cooper as my Interceptor screams official vehicle. We park near the maintenance building that gives us a view of the entrance.

At 7:45 Mr. Alexander arrives in his white Mercedes. He parks next to the first of two ponds and gets out. After looking around the well-lit area and noting the spattering of people here for nighttime exercise, a few families lingering on the playground, and a softball game winding down, he chooses a private bench under an oak tree.

At 7:55 Judge Aaron arrives driving a silver four-door Jeep. He parks next to the Mercedes and joins Alexander at the bench. They don't speak. They don't even look at each other. Aaron remains standing and Alexander stays seated on the bench.

Five minutes later, a mint green VW Beetle pulls in. A

young woman steps out dressed grunge with ripped jeans, a flannel, and Doc Martens. She slams the driver's door before strutting over to join them.

Mr. Alexander stands.

The young woman folds her arms, glaring at him.

He hands her an envelope. She snags it and hurls it toward the pond. It lands on the grassy bank. Roughly, Ronan grabs her. He says something. She wrenches away, shoving him. Mr. Alexander steps forward, calmly reaching out. She slaps him. He doesn't move.

Ronan grabs her again, this time even harder. He shakes her. "What is wrong with you?" he yells.

"Let me go!" she screams.

Maybe it's everything going on with Tyler, my emotional connection to Ronan, or my earlier conversation with the sheriff, but I'm out of the Mini Cooper and charging toward them before I think it through.

"Nell," Vaughn hisses.

I ignore him.

My shoes eat up the ground, quickly covering the distance between us and them. "Hey!" I shout. "Let her go."

All three turn to stare. Ronan's hand falls away. Alexander's eyes narrow. The girl blinks. I come up right in their personal space. Now that I'm closer, I see the girl is a little older than I initially thought—nineteen or twenty.

"Who the hell are you?" she snaps.

I flash my badge.

"Oh, this is priceless." She laughs.

My glare moves over them. "What is going on?"

"Nell," Ronan sighs.

Alexander shakes his head. "You are going to regret this."

"I doubt it."

Vaughn comes up beside me. The girl gives him an appreciative once-over as he walks over to the pond and retrieves the five-by-seven envelope that landed a few inches away from the water.

"What is going on?" I repeat.

Both men remain silent. The girl looks between them. She throws her hands up. "Fine, you're the one with secrets. Not me." Her voice raises. "I don't care if the whole world knows!"

Holding up a hand, Ronan steps forward. "Nell, this is Kinsley Aaron, my baby sister. We only recently found out that Ian is her father. We are understandably overwhelmed and trying to work through this. It's not exactly an issue we're ready for everyone to know about."

A silent beat goes by. I don't look at Mr. Alexander because I know he's about to reign down his ire on me and the whole damn department. "Is that what you two were arguing about Sunday night?"

"How do you know about that?" Ian snaps.

I do look at him now. As expected, he looks furious.

Ronan saves me from mentioning the eyewitness who flaked when he says, "Yes. Kinsley showed up over there drunk. She passed out in a lounge chair. I went to get her."

"What time was that?"

"About ten at night."

"Where was your son?"

"Asleep in the back of my Jeep."

"Was the tan Nissan there or gone at this time?"

"I don't know. I was in such a hurry, I wasn't paying attention to whether or not cars were in their spots."

Vaughn still holds the envelope. Kinsley takes it from him and opens it up. She pulls out a passport with hundred-dollar bills stacked neatly inside. She waves it in front of

Ian's face. "Actually, I will take this. Thank you very much, *Daddy*." Next, she brings out plane tickets. "And I'll say yes to this. You want to get rid of me? Fine, I'll go."

"I'm not trying to get rid of you." Mr. Alexander steps toward her. "I know how much you want to see Europe. That's me helping you do that. That's all. We'll figure this out, Kinsley. I promise."

She shoots him a dirty look, then flounces over to her car, gets in, and revs off into the night.

Ian watches her go. When she's clear from the park and her car disappears down the road, he turns on me. "You, Detective Nell Brach, are over."

He's right, I probably am. I'm already in so deep, I might as well ask one last question. I look at Ronan. "Mrs. Alexander dropped Scarlett Macadem at your house Sunday at approximately five thirty. How could you not have known she was there?"

"It's a big property. If she didn't ring the doorbell to the main house..." He shrugs. "I don't know what to tell you. At that time I was in the den in an all-out Nintendo battle with my son."

"To clarify, you did not see her?"

"No," Ronan says. "I did not."

I hate that I'm not sure if I believe him.

THIRTY-FOUR

Friday, 8:45 a.m.

I DIDN'T SLEEP. I was out the door before the sun came up. I went for a run in the park, thinking about everything—the case, my brother, the meeting last night. What a shit show that was.

I showered at the station.

I've been at my desk for hours when Vaughn walks in.

Today he wears a retro robot tie with black chinos and gray cowboy boots. I wear my usual ensemble. I'm the person who would've done well in a school uniform. I'm not much for variety.

"You didn't sleep," he notices.

"Nope."

"Anything you want to talk about aside from the case?"

"Nope."

He nods toward the break room, and I follow him down the hall. While he makes green tea, I fish a Greek yogurt from the refrigerator.

"Any thoughts on the photo leak?" he asks.

I spoon up some yogurt and eat. "I know who it is and it has been dealt with."

"Should we tell the sheriff?" He gives me a curious look.

"No." I eat more yogurt. "I've handled it."

"Okay." Vaughn blows on his green tea before sipping.

One more bite of yogurt and I throw it away. "You should know Owens delivered an ultimatum. One more mistake and he's taking over."

"Oh."

"And that was before last night's debacle." I pour coffee and add coconut milk. It's my third cup.

"I know you don't want to hear this, but you should probably give Ian Alexander an apology. He's not involved in this, and though I've been here less than a week, I already know he can make your life miserable."

"I don't care."

"Yes, you do. Once your pissy mood lifts, you'll see that. You have your whole career ahead of you. Eating a little bit of crow isn't going to kill you. I'm not saying you need to grovel. But a professional apology is in order. Sooner rather than later before he places a call to Sheriff Owens."

"He may have already," I grumble.

While Vaughn goes about making oatmeal in the microwave, I take my coffee back to my desk.

I hate to admit it, but my partner's right. I'm just starting out. This is my first lead case. Despite crossing those t's and dotting i's, I'm still screwing up. Perhaps being the lead detective is motivating me in the wrong way. Am I trying too hard to make a name for myself instead of focusing on what's important—Scarlett Macadem?

I'd like to think I'm humble, but the truth is, my confidence borders cockiness. Being the youngest and only female detective doesn't help. It fuels that arrogance. Yet a level of that is needed to be a good investigator. It's the balance that matters. I know this; I simply haven't learned it. That balance comes from experience, and I am on the left side of that bell curve for sure.

With a deep breath, I sink into my chair and close my eyes. My mind drifts to Sunday night. I imagine the scene. Mrs. Alexander drops Scarlett off. She looks around for her uncle. Perhaps she walks up the exterior steps to his garage apartment. But he's not there. She sees the "Gone Fishing" sign hanging on his door. She tries the knob anyway. It's locked. She's been there before. She knows her way around. She notes all the cars are in their spots, which means Judge Aaron should be home. She descends the exterior steps. Maybe she walks to the back door of the main house where she knocks. But no one answers. Inside Ronan and his son are playing loud video games. They don't hear her. She could wait for her uncle or she could—

My eyes open. On my phone, I do an aerial shot of Ronan's address. I zoom out, studying the surrounding area.

Carrying his oatmeal, Vaughn sits down at his desk. He takes a bite. "What are you looking at?"

"Scarlett's backpack was full of everything she needed to stay the night with Elle. The security footage from the town carnival showed her getting into Bennett Alexander's Land Rover without a backpack. Somewhere between him dropping her at the courthouse and her being in the back of that car, she got it back. How?" I show Vaughn my phone, pointing to a neighborhood just one mile from Aaron's home. "That's where Elle Psaltis lives."

THIRTY-FIVE

Friday, 10 a.m.

THE PSALTIS FAMILY lives in a new cookie-cutter type of neighborhood for mid-income households. Neatly maintained by the HOA, there's a section for townhomes and an area for single-family units. We pull into a house painted light green with dark green shutters. In the driveway sits a red Subaru.

I ring the doorbell.

"Coming!" Mrs. Psaltis yells.

A few seconds later, the door opens. Still dressed in pajamas with no makeup, she has her thin dark hair held back on both sides with bobby pins.

She looks down at her matching striped sleepwear. "Sorry, I'm usually dressed by now."

I note a slight discoloration under her right eye. "What happened there?"

"Oh, um..." Her hand comes up. Lightly, her fingers touch the bruise. "I fell. I know how that sounds. But I did."

"Hm."

She clears her throat. "How can I help you?"

"We need to ask you a few follow-up questions," Vaughn says. "Elle too if she's here."

"Elle's at school. But I'll answer what I can." She steps aside, letting us into an immaculately cleaned living room that looks more like an Ethan Allen showroom than a home. "Do you mind taking off your shoes? I don't care, but my husband does."

We oblige. She offers us a beverage that we decline. We sit around an L-shaped white sofa.

Nervously, she looks between us. "Is this about what Elle did with that boy?"

"No, it's not," I say.

This seems to help her relax.

"Mrs. Psaltis, when you picked Scarlett up from her home on Sunday, did she have a backpack with her?"

"Yes."

"When you dropped the girls off at the school carnival, did she take the backpack with her?"

"No, she left it in my car. When I got home, I brought it in the house and took it to Elle's room."

"What time did you pick Elle up from the carnival?"

She looks away, thinking about that. "Probably like six? Elle texted me that she was ready to come home. I left here and drove into town. Elle told me Scarlett's mom had already picked her up. I didn't think anything about it. Elle said she was hungry. We went through KFC and came home after that."

"Putting you back here at what time?"

"I'd say seven."

"Can we see Elle's room?"

"Sure." She shows us from the living room, down a

Berber-carpeted hall, and into a girl's bedroom decorated with maple wood furniture, light purple walls, and carpet that matches the hall. She points to an empty corner. "I put it there. I didn't realize until just now that it was gone. Have you found it?"

"Yes, we found it on Sunday at the rock quarry."

She frowns. "That doesn't make sense."

"Does Scarlett have a key to your home?"

"No." She points to a window. "But the girls come and go from there. I've never cared. They think it's fun." From the other side of the house, a timer dings. "I have to check that. I'll be right back."

Mrs. Psaltis hurries from Elle's room. While Vaughn examines the window, I walk over to a corkboard hanging above a maple wood desk. Pictures cover it—some of the two girls at school, a few vacation-type of shots, but most of Scarlett's family. There's Mrs. Macadem in the kitchen with the girls. Mr. Macadem laughing as he points a water gun. Elle tickling the twins. Scarlett and her parents blowing matching pink bubbles. And various others. None are of Elle's parents.

She wanted to be part of Scarlett's family so very much.

"Easy enough," my partner says.

I look over to see him standing outside, looking in the open window. He closes it and easily opens it right back up. "No screen, no engaged lock. She came here, got her backpack, and then left."

Mrs. Psaltis returns. "Do you think she took Elle's bike then? Because we can't find it."

THIRTY-SIX

Friday, 11:15 a.m.

I GIVE Mrs. Psaltis my card, telling her to call any time should she have another "fall."

As I drive away from her house, I say, "Now that Scarlett's got a bike, her radius grows. Where would she go?"

"Back to Depot Hill?" On his phone, Vaughn launches a map.

"That's fifteen-plus miles. She needs someplace closer to hang out while she waits on her uncle to return from fishing."

"The sun sets at 7:15. According to Mrs. Psaltis, the bike does not have a light. That leaves Scarlett roughly an hour of daylight to kill."

My phone rings. It's Ophelia. Over Bluetooth, I answer. "Hi."

"I am *so* sorry. I heard about what happened. Judge Aaron and Mr. Alexander were in here this morning talking about it."

"You were right in coming to us."

"I want you to know that I take full responsibility. I told the judge and Mr. Alexander that I was the reason why you and Detective London showed up at the park."

"Ophelia, you did not need to do that."

"I had to! Mr. Alexander was fired up. He was ready to call in every favor to get you kicked off the force."

The yogurt I ate hours ago sours in my stomach.

"When he left here, he was much calmer. I now know what the big secret is. I am such a fool. I am truly sorry, Nell. Would you like me to call the sheriff and explain I was the catalyst?"

"No, but thank you. Is everything okay on your end? With your job, I mean?"

"Well, given I can retire if I want, I'm not worried. However, the judge and I are going to speak privately about it later."

"Will you keep me in the loop?"

"Of course."

We hang up.

Vaughn turns the phone for me to see. He points to a series of buildings, trailing his finger two miles down to Elle's, one mile up to Aaron, and then back to form a triangle. It's the hospital where Scarlett volunteers for school credit.

THIRTY-SEVEN

Friday, noon

"WE'RE ALL SO sad about Scarlett," the pediatric nurse says. "A few of us went over to her home yesterday to pay our respects."

"That was kind of you," I say.

The nurse smiles sadly. Vaughn wanders down the hall of the children's ward.

I ask, "How many days per week did she come and what type of things did she do?"

"She was here Tuesday after school and would come Saturday in the late morning." The nurse nods into a play-room. "Mostly she was there, reading to the kids or playing with them."

"Did you work this past Sunday?"

"No. But—" she stops another nurse who is walking past. "You worked Sunday. Did you see Scarlett?"

"I did briefly, yes." The other nurse nods down the hall. "She checked in on her favorite patient."

"What time was this?" I ask.

"Around six thirty. I get my dinner break then and I had just warmed up some leftover stir-fry. That's the only reason why I know."

"What room is her favorite patient in?"

"One-zero-two," the first nurse answers. "You're welcome to peek in, but if she's not up and awake, please don't bother her. She had a round of chemo today. It's most important she rests."

"Of course."

After thanking them both, I walk to room 102. The door is open. Quietly, I step in. With yellow walls and two beds, the dimly lit room smells of antiseptic and baby powder. A door to the left opens into a private bathroom, dark and empty. A crème-colored pleather sleeping lounge takes up the corner. To the right, the first of two beds is empty. A little girl with a bald head sleeps soundly in the second bed, her arms snug around a floppy stuffed bunny. She looks to be around five years old. On the table beside her bed sits a glass bowl half full of pink pom-poms. They're the same pom-poms we found in Scarlett's backpack.

On the wall above the girl's bed, a few scenic sketches have been taped. Even from where I stand in the doorway, I recognize the skill level of the artist. One of the rock quarry on a starry night draws my attention.

"Hey," Vaughn whispers from behind me. "I've got something."

Back out in the hall, I find the same nurse. "I noticed the bowl of pink pom-poms."

"That was Scarlett's idea. June wants to grow up to be a cheerleader. Every time she did something brave, Scarlett put a pom-pom in that bowl. Once the bowl is full, the plan was to do a slumber party with movies and junk food." With a sigh, she looks away from me toward June's room. "Guess we need to keep doing that."

"And the sketches?"

"Scarlett's quite the artist. You'll find her drawings all over the pediatric ward. We plan on leaving them up, of course. The kids love them." A beeping from the nurse's station draws her attention. She excuses herself.

Vaughn says, "I found the security office. They're pulling all the video footage from Sunday evening. They're going to email it to us."

"Perfect."

THIRTY-EIGHT

Friday, 1:15 p.m.

WE MAKE a quick stop at the hospital cafeteria for sandwiches to go.

As we're leaving the hospital, we run into Mr. Alexander. I'm tempted to pretend I don't see him, but I opt to be mature instead.

After beeping the lock on his Mercedes, he simultaneously checks his phone as he walks toward the main entrance.

I stand where I am, waiting.

"Want me to scram?" Vaughn asks.

"No, it's fine."

Mr. Alexander comes to a halt when he sees us. He holds up a hand, sarcastically saying, "I'm here for a board meeting."

My God, I do not like this man. But, it's time for me to eat some crow. "I spoke with Judge Aaron's secretary. I know you're aware of how I ended up at the park. I wanted to apologize for intruding on a private family matter."

"Is that all you want to apologize for?"

Dick.

Vaughn clears his throat.

"Being good at my job means I'm going to ask a lot of questions, follow leads that may end nowhere, and occasionally piss people off. All of these things I have done with you. This is me recognizing that. Thank you for your time." I step around him and walk away before I verbalize every cuss word known to man.

"Detective Brach?"

My eyes close. I was so close to getting out of here with my temper in check. I turn back.

"I don't have proof, but I'm pretty damn sure my wife and Gerald Macadem are having an affair."

Yep, I could've told him that.

"I think they were together Sunday night. If you can prove it, I'd like to know." With that, he walks off.

"Relationship goals," Vaughn mutters.

"Mrs. Alexander's mother said she last saw her daughter at nine on Sunday night before waking and seeing her Monday morning. That's a whole night's worth of hours she could've come and gone from that place." I fish my keys out. "Let's take a drive to that mother-daughter spa."

"Ian dropped that nugget for divorce reasons. They're both working the prenup void angle."

"Maybe, but it did twinge something in my gut."

"You got a gut twinge?" He slides his Ray-Bans on. "Sounds serious."

THIRTY-NINE

Friday, 3 p.m.

I NAVIGATE up a steep mountain road and pull into a circular drive with valet parking.

I show my badge. "The car stays here."

"Yes, ma'am." With a nod, the valet backs away to open a thick, brass-and-wood door.

Side by side we stand in an elegant gold and stone lobby with floor-to-ceiling glass windows that look out over the Smoky Mountains.

A mellow voice greets us. "Hello, welcome. Do you have a reservation?"

I turn to see a young woman behind the check-in desk. I have never described someone as having a peaceful aura, but this woman has it. She seems to glow. Or that could just be the moon lamp on the desk in front of her.

Vaughn shows his badge. "We need to speak with your head of security."

"Certainly," she calmly replies.

While we wait, I take a lap around the lobby. Vaughn does the same. I pass a small bar with opened wine bottles and three water dispensers—one infused with sliced cucumber, another with lemon, and the last with strawberries.

I help myself to the cucumber one.

Large potted ferns separate clumps of leather lounge chairs. Two women sit chatting, silhouetted by the Smokies' peaks and valleys, and sharing a bottle of white wine.

I'm not sure I would do well in a place like this. I'm not good at relaxing.

I note the security camera mounted in the top corner, pointed at the entrance. Perfect.

"Detective?" Dressed in a suit and tie, a man I'd place in his fifties approaches my partner standing by the enormous windows. I join them.

We both show him our credentials.

I point to the corner-mounted camera. "We need the footage from that starting Sunday at five p.m. and going twelve hours forward."

No expression crosses his face. "What is this about?"

"A dead girl," I say.

"Sorry to disappoint, but our footage erases every twenty-four hours."

"That's convenient." I look around the lobby. "Then we'll start with whoever was working Sunday night." I nod to the receptionist. "Was she?"

He smiles tightly. "Unless you have a warrant, you need to leave."

FORTY

Friday, 3:45 p.m.

"WHY DID I know that would happen?" I navigate back down the mountain.

"Maybe if you had better people skills," Vaughn says as he reads something on his phone.

I ignore my partner's sarcasm. "We won't be able to get a warrant, not for the spa. We do have the footage from the hospital. Let's get back to the station and review that. I also want to walk the hospital ward and look at all the sketches Scarlett did. Though we'll probably need to do that during the morning when the children are awake and having breakfast. I noticed one of the rock quarry. It didn't seem accurate. It looked more like a generic quarry at night. Also—"

"Actually, if you don't mind, I need to clock out for the day."

I look over at him. He's still reading whatever is on his phone. "Actually, I *do* mind." My tone comes harsher than I intended. It surprises me.

"I'll be in tomorrow morning," he patiently replies.

"I thought you 'didn't have a life.'"

He doesn't reply, just keeps reading whatever is on his screen.

I resist the urge to grab it from his fingers. "*What* do you keep looking at? And where do you have to go that's more important than this?"

"Not that it's your business, but I have a meeting with someone. I said I'll be in tomorrow morning. First thing." Now he's the one with the snappy tone.

"Yeah, well, it's my business when we're on an active investigation."

He doesn't reply. Instead, he puts his phone away and looks out the side window, watching the trees roll past.

Fine, whatever.

I concentrate on driving the steep mountain road as it cuts back and forth. The air between us constricts with irritation. Vaughn looked into me. It's time I looked into him.

"Wait, pull over." He points to the right where a country store sits on the side of the mountain bracketed in by thick pines. "They've got a security camera at their gas pump."

"This road is the only way in and out of the spa." I smirk. "Good catch."

"*So* glad you're happy," he murmurs.

INSIDE THE COUNTRY STORE, the elderly woman working the counter is also the owner. In a pleasant southern-belle accent, she doesn't hesitate, "Oh my goodness, of course, I'll help. I heard all about that poor girl. I don't know how to pull the footage off our camera, but my husband does. Give me some time to track him down, and we'll send you our Sunday night film. No problem."

Perfect. I give her my contact information.

FORTY-ONE

Friday, 8:15 p.m.

BLEARY-EYED I CONTINUE FLICKING through the hundreds of still photos and hours of video taken by the hospital security cameras. If there's a way to sort everything, I haven't figured it out. So far, I've seen still shots and footage of the ER, the ICU, the maternity ward, the admin area, the exterior, the interior, the morgue, and on and on. Scarlett is in none of them.

I could sure use Vaughn.

Blowing out a breath, I sit back and close my eyes. I roll my neck. I stand up and stretch.

In the break room, I consider coffee and choose water instead. I make myself stand right here and drink an entire bottle. After tossing it into the recycle, I go to the bathroom. I don't want to, but I look at myself in the mirror. From the shadows under my bloodshot brown eyes, dry lips, and pale face to my limp ponytail, I look like I need to sleep for ten straight hours.

Because I do.

But I don't want to go home and deal with Mom and Tyler. I don't have it in me.

Instead, I do my thing in the bathroom and go back to my desk. If I look at one more picture of the hospital, I might scream.

I choose to research Vaughn instead.

Minutes later, I'm a total creeper hunched over my laptop reading the words that describe Vaughn London's worst night, dated seven years ago.

Woman and child killed, one injured in DUI crash that closed I-40 in Nashville.

Driver arrested by troopers faces DUI charges in a fatal wreck. A Murfreesboro man was arrested in connection with a crash on I-40 in Davidson County that killed a Nashville woman, her unborn child, and seriously injured one passenger, her husband.

According to the crash report, the 40-year-old Murfreesboro man—identified as Henry John Kelly —was driving a truck south in the inside lane. The Nashville couple was driving a sedan in the center lane.

Troopers said the truck entered the sedan's lane and collided with it, causing it to rotate, strike and travel over a guardrail, before overturning. The sedan's passenger suffered fatal injuries, dying later at the hospital. The sedan's driver, a 26-year-old male, was injured in the crash. Kelly was unharmed and taken to the Davidson County jail. He faces charges of DUI, manslaughter, and property damage.

Seven years ago, I was fighting for Tyler's life at the same time Vaughn was battling for his wife and unborn child. How horrible.

Next, I type in "Henry John Kelly, Davidson County." A mug shot pops up of a heavy man with short black hair, splotchy skin, and red-rimmed eyes. I read a notice dated one year ago:

Parole denied for Murfreesboro man convicted in DUI fatality

Henry John Kelly, 45, attended a hearing with the Tennessee Department of Corrections and Rehabilitation's parole board. He has so far served five years of a 10-year sentence. Kelly struck and killed a Nashville woman and her unborn child during a DUI incident.

The parole board attributed its decision to the crash having involved substance abuse, the death of an unborn child, and the deceased's husband who spoke in front of the parole board in an emotionally moving speech. Kelly will re-petition in one year.

Sheriff Owens steps from his office. He sees me at my desk and walks over. I close the laptop.

"Missed your brother today," he says.

"Mom spent it with him. You understand."

"Of course." He surveys Vaughn's empty desk and the sparsely manned workroom. "You should go home. Get a fresh start in the morning. Not to be rude, but you look like shit."

I chuckle. "Thanks. I have security footage to review, then I'll go home."

"From?"

"The hospital. We've confirmed Scarlett was there Sunday night. We're trying to establish a timeline and where she went from there. Don't suppose we can get a warrant for a spa in Gatlinburg?"

"Not unless you can put Scarlett there."

"No." My twingy gut aside, at this point, it's more mari-tal-based. "It's okay, we've got other footage coming in. By the way, did you hear from Ian Alexander today?"

"I did not. Should I have?"

"Nope, just curious." I reopen my laptop.

Stepping forward, he closes it. "I was serious. Go home to your mom and Tyler. Get some rest. You look strung out."

FORTY-TWO

Friday, 9:05 p.m.

WHEN I WALK into my home, I find Olivia, Grace and Luca's mom, sitting on the couch next to my mom. They're huddled like they've been talking quietly. Tension fills the room.

"What's going on?" I ask.

Mom looks up at me, and though she hasn't been crying, it's clear she hasn't had a good day. Quietly, she says, "Tyler hasn't talked to me the entire day. He's barely even come out of his room."

"Why didn't you call me?"

"Because, Nell, you're not his mother. I am. I should be able to handle this. Yet, I don't know what to do." She lets out a humorless laugh. "Did I really think I would come back and he would be my little boy again?"

"Mom..."

Shaking her head, she looks at her best friend. "Olivia's

offered me her extra room, and I've accepted. Until Tyler and I can reestablish a relationship, it's for the best."

"Mom, no."

She stands and hugs me. "I'll just be on the other side of the trees. It's not like I'm moving back to Georgia."

It's then I notice she's already packed and placed one box and one suitcase near the front door. Shit, she's leaving.

With a kiss on my cheek, she nods to Olivia, and the two each grab Mom's things. At the door, she looks back. "I love you. I'll see you this weekend."

Then, she leaves.

For several minutes I stand still in the living room with its thin carpet, worn furniture, and frayed curtains. I expect to feel fresh anger at my brother for forcing Mom to leave. Instead, I feel...relief.

And that brings guilt.

I want Mom here. I do. I just don't know how to manage what it's doing to Tyler. This has been a rough week, and I don't think it all has to do with Mom.

After hanging my windbreaker on the wall mount and prying off my hiking shoes, I walk the hall to Tyler's room. I knock. "Tyler?"

"Come in."

I open the door to find him on the floor with his legs stretched long on the wall. He looks away from the book he's reading and directly at my gun. I usually put it in my safe as soon as I get home.

Lying down beside him, I stretch my legs up next to his. I stare at my striped socks. So does he.

"Mom's gone," I say. "She's moving in with Olivia."

"Oh."

"I tore you a new one yesterday, didn't I?"

"Yep." Closing his book, he places it on the floor. "I deserved it."

"What's going on, Tyler? First with the pot, then with the photo." I look over at him. "Not to mention the bombshell you've secretly been emailing with Dad."

"I don't know." Tears fill his eyes.

"Hey." I grip his thigh. "What's going on?"

Sniffing, he brushes them away. "It's just hard, ya know?" More tears. "No one likes me, Nell. I hate school. I hate it so much." His bottom lip wobbles. "Hell, the only person who ever really smiled at me in the halls was Scarlett. Now she's gone, and what did I do? I dug through your phone and emailed that photo to play a goddamn stupid game because I thought it would—" his voice cracks— "make me popular or something." He covers his face. "I'm an asshole," he whispers.

My heart cracks.

Rolling over, I wrap my arm around him, and I hold him while he cries. I had no idea he hated school so much. I don't say anything. I simply hug him while he rides through the emotion.

Eventually, he sniffs and wipes his nose with his T-shirt. "Sometimes I just want to disappear."

My body stills. He's never talked like that before.

"Not like what you're thinking, Nell. More, I wish I could run far away and never come back to this town."

"I get that." *Sometimes people run, so others will come looking,* Grandpa said that to me once. "Know that if you ever run, your big sister will come looking, and I will find you."

"It's not you that I want to hide from. It's everybody else."

"If there's one thing I've learned, it's that a 'fresh start' isn't all it's cracked up to be. Sometimes it's best to stay put and make use of what you've got. That said, we can talk about school. There are options. Let me noodle it around. Bottom line, I want you to enjoy school, not hate it. You hate it. Let's see if we can change that."

He blows out a relieved breath. "Thanks."

"You're welcome."

"I need to give you the email address that I sent the photo to. You need to find out who's on the other end. That stupid game should be stopped."

"Agreed."

He sniffs and wipes his nose. "I'm going to need a new T-shirt."

"Listen, I am one hundred percent okay with you and Dad. He's your father. If you want a relationship with him, you should have one. Just because I have a bad taste in my mouth about the man, doesn't mean you should." I sit up. "Don't feel like you need to hide it from me, though, okay?"

"Okay."

"Let's make a promise to talk about that 'fresh start' again in a year. I'm not closing the idea down; I'm just asking for a year. Let's get your school figured out and see how you feel in twelve months. Deal?"

"Deal."

"Also, and I know you don't want to hear this, but it'd be great if you give Mom a chance. I'm not trying to make you feel guilty, but she was in that place because of what happened to you and Luca. You know this. She loves you, as do I. We would do anything for you."

One last sniff and he sits up. "I know. It's just…" Reaching over, he fiddles with the book. "That's part of the problem at school. Everyone knows my mom was locked up in a mental hospital."

"What about Luca?"

"What about him?" Tyler mumbles.

"What's he like at school?"

"He's popular." He keeps fiddling with the book. "Everyone likes him."

"Does he not talk to you?"

My brother scoffs. "Hell, he's the one who keeps reminding everyone my mom's crazy."

FORTY-THREE

Saturday, 8:45 a.m.

I LEAVE Tyler at home with a promise to check in with me every hour. When I walk into the station, I find Vaughn already sitting at his desk, reviewing the hospital security footage.

"Morning." I slide out of my windbreaker and loop it over the back of my chair.

"Morning," he replies, not looking at me.

I sit down at my desk. "I was an asshole to you yesterday. I've had a lot thrown at me this week, and I haven't been handling the stress well. No excuse, but know that I'm sorry."

Vaughn looks up from his laptop. "Apology accepted."

"Thank you." Today he wears a black and green dinosaur tie. I nod to it. "Cute."

"I try." He sits back, folding his hands over his flat abs. "Anything you want to talk about?"

I would rather do anything other than talk, but something about his calm demeanor and that silly tie has me saying, "I never know how to handle my brother. He's not had it easy. I know it's important to establish routines and rules, but he's such a different kid than I was. He's got this emotional and tender side that I've never had. I don't want to break what tiny spirit he has. He's so beaten down by life. This week in particular has been especially challenging. He's been even more withdrawn and did a few things way out of character. But we had a good talk last night, and I think we've rounded a corner. At least now I know the root of his despondency." Picking up a pencil, I tap the eraser end on my desk. "Sometimes I wonder what kind of young man he would've turned out to be if he wasn't taken as a child."

"Same goes with you, I imagine. Who would you be right now if all of that hadn't happened?"

Good question. "I'd still be a detective, I think. I certainly wouldn't be living with my brother. I probably would not be getting along with my mom. That's the one good thing to come out of this, I have a respect and appreciation for her I never had before."

"That's good."

I try to spin the pencil like Tyler does, but it rolls off my knuckles and across the desk. "Well, anyway..."

"Bottom line, a kid needs love and stability and someone to show the hell up."

"Tyler's got that with me, no question."

"What I want to know is, who shows up for you?"

That throws me off. No one has ever asked me that before.

"Seems to me you spend a lot of time taking care of your mom and your brother. Who takes care of you?"

No one. I've always taken care of myself.

Vaughn smiles knowingly. "Looks like I've rendered Detective Brach mute."

I let out a nervous laugh.

A few awkward beats go by.

I need the attention off of me. He's going to know I've been snooping, but I still say, "I'm sorry to hear about your wife and child."

"Now look who has excellent detective skills."

"Are you okay?"

"I don't know. He's up for parole again in two weeks. My lawyer and I have been exchanging messages all week. She was in the area on other business. That's who I met with last night. She wants me to speak again at his hearing."

"Are you?"

"Maybe. I need to think about it. It took a lot out of me last year. Emotionally, I'm not sure I can do it again. Just when I get myself back in a good head space, something comes up that reminds me about everything that I lost. Like this parole thing."

I think of last night's conversation with my brother. "You came here from Nashville for a fresh start. I know it's only been a week, but do you feel it was the right decision?"

"Yes, no doubt."

The only thing that's been keeping me in this area is Mom. Now that she's out, I do have the freedom to move me and Tyler should I choose. It would be easy enough to take Mom with us, should she want. It would require some paperwork and a talk with her probation officer. Or at least I think. I'd have to check.

As if reading my brain, Vaughn says, "I just got here. Do a man a solid and don't hand me off to another partner."

"I won't." A smile curves through my face. I nod to his laptop. "Any luck?"

"Yes." He turns it around.

There's a black and white photo stamped at 7:30 p.m. on Sunday. It was taken outside the hospital's main entrance. Though it's dark out, Scarlett and a male nurse climb into a maroon-colored SUV with a Lyft sticker.

Vaughn zooms in on the license plate.

Gotcha.

FORTY-FOUR

Saturday, 10:15 a.m.

ON THE WAY to the Lyft driver's address, my phone rings over Bluetooth. "Tyler, hi, you're on speaker in my car. Vaughn's here."

"Hey, Tyler," my partner greets him.

"Our cheese has green on it," my brother tells me.

Vaughn and I share an amused look.

"Just cut it off," Vaughn says. "You'll be fine."

"Really?"

"I do it all the time," he assures him.

"Okay, but if I come down with some rare microbial funk, I'm blaming you."

"Duly noted."

After a round of byes, I hang up. He sounds in a much better spirit today.

A few minutes later, we pull in next to a maroon SUV.

The Lyft driver lives in a newly renovated brick and wood apartment building with six units—three on the bottom and three on top. Her door sits first on the left. I knock. Seconds later a woman around my age answers.

With two long light brown braids, a green mask on her face, and dressed in sweatpants and a tank top, she smiles widely. It's a smile that lights up her entire masked face. It's a smile that makes me smile.

"Hi," she says. "Can I help you?"

"Charlotte Swift?" I ask. She nods. We both show her our badges. "We need to ask you a few questions."

"Oh goodness." She cringes. "Did I run a red light or something? Oh, I hope not."

"No." Vaughn smiles too. "You're not in any trouble. It won't take long. Wouldn't want to interfere with your beauty routine."

Charlotte giggles.

"You can come in but fair warning, I'm doing a bit of spring cleaning. The place is a mess." She waves us in, and she's not kidding—from buckets and spray bottles, to dusters and a vacuum, to upended furniture and multiple piles of laundry—she's not just spring cleaning, she's tackling the other seasons as well.

After righting a few couch cushions, she motions us to sit. "Are you thirsty? I don't have much but you're welcome to what I have, which is probably just water and instant coffee if I'm being honest."

"We're fine," I tell her.

Vaughn pulls up the photo of Scarlett. "Did you give this girl a ride on Sunday?"

"I sure did! Cute little thing. She was with a man. At first, I thought it was her daddy or something but I learned he was just riding with her. He had on scrubs, so I guess he was probably a doctor or a nurse. They must've known each other well. They were laughing and talking the whole time. Even broke into a round of nursery rhyme songs."

"Where did you take them?" I ask.

"Two stops." Charlotte holds up a finger. "Let me get my phone." She disappears down a hall and is back in seconds, already scrolling the Lyft app. She sits back down. "Yep, two stops." She hands us the phone.

I note the first one was Ronan Aaron's home with a drop-off time of 8:16. The second was a neighborhood some miles away at 8:29. "Who did you drop off first?"

"The young girl. Then I took the man to his home. I guess he was riding with her to make sure she got home safe. It was his account that ordered and paid for the ride."

"Did she have a bike with her?" Vaughn asks.

"No, she had a backpack though. I do remember them talking about a flat tire. She asked the man if he was sure the bike would be safe overnight." Charlotte shrugs. "Maybe the bike's at the hospital. That's where I picked them up. Is that what this is about? Did someone file a report on a missing bike?"

I note her green mask is starting to dry and turn a paler shade. "Do you want to wash your face? We'll wait."

"Nah." She waves that off. "If you all don't mind my freaky state, I certainly don't care."

"Did you see anything when you dropped the girl off?" Vaughn asks. "Other people, for example, other cars, weird lights, did you hear any sounds..."

"No, the place was well lit but I didn't see anybody. Great house. She told me to pull around back because that was where her uncle lived. She directed me to stop at a garage. The man who was with her asked if she was sure her uncle was home. She said he'd be home any minute. Let me think..." Her big green eyes look up and to the left. "Oh! As

I pulled away, I checked my rearview and saw her walking into the garage."

"Not up the exterior steps?" I ask.

"No, the garage is one of those open ones. There were two cars parked. Or rather one car, and a truck. She walked between the two of them and got into the car."

Vaughn and I exchange a look.

"What do you mean she got into the car?" he asks.

"The driver's side. I figured it was her uncle's car and she was just going to hang out and wait on him. Then I took the man to his home. I had a few more rides that night and eventually clocked out." She looks between us. "I've never been questioned by cops before. How'd I do? Do I get to ask what this is about or is it top secret?"

I don't have the heart to tell her she's one of the last people to see Scarlett alive. Instead, I give Charlotte my contact information, tell her to call if she remembers anything else, and leave her to her spring cleaning.

———

"I WISH all people I question were that easy." Back in the vehicle, I start the engine, but I don't drive off. "Gerald Macadem got home roughly forty-five minutes later. He said the car was still there. Scarlett's time of death is eleven p.m. That's two hours. Where was Scarlett when he got home? The Lyft driver said she got in his car on the driver's side."

"Did she fall asleep waiting on her uncle?"

"Or did she purposefully wait for him to get home and settled in his apartment before taking a little joy ride? She'd been there enough to know where the keys are."

"Okay, let's say she went for that joy ride," Vaughn says.

"She's thirteen. The rock quarry is fifteen miles from Judge Aaron's home. It's dark out. Why go to the quarry? And how does she know how to drive?"

"Unless her Uncle Gerald taught her..."

"That doesn't explain the Rohypnol in her system."

"You found a party spot at the quarry." I look over at him. "Maybe something was going on she wanted to be part of. She drove the car there. Whoever was partying offered her a drink laced with Rohypnol. Then why wasn't she violated? Why give her the date rape drug if you're not going to rape her?"

Vaughn slides his Ray-Bans on. "Are we back to The Quiet Game? 'Drink this and climb in the back of the car. And oh, by the way, we're going to push you in the water and see if you can escape. All while not making a sound.'"

"As ridiculous as that sounds, unfortunately, I can see it playing out."

"Me too."

I put the car in reverse and back out. As I drive away, a call comes in from an unknown number. "Detective Brach here. May I help you?"

"Hi, you came by my store yesterday and asked for the footage from the camera above our gas pump. My husband is here and he has it. How do we get it to you?"

I give her my email address, thank her, and hang up.

FORTY-FIVE

Saturday, noon

GERALD MACADEM HAS TEMPORARILY MOVED BACK into his childhood home—a two-story, peach-painted one with white shutters situated in one of White Quail's oldest neighborhoods. I pull in behind the vintage red Cadillac and park. It's the only vehicle in the driveway.

We navigate along a small walkway lined with neatly trimmed bushes and up onto a front porch with wicker furniture. Vaughn rings the bell. Gerald answers quickly, like he was standing just on the other side of the door.

He looks between us. "I was just on my way out." He holds up a list. "Mom asked me to do the grocery shopping."

"This won't take long." I step into the house, giving him no chance *not* to invite us in.

"My parents are both gone," he says like he's a teenager still and not a grown-ass man.

"We're here to talk to you." I nod to the left where a formal dining room sits. "Let's speak in there."

After we're situated around a glass-topped table big enough to comfortably hold six people, Vaughn says, "We're going to need you to walk us through Sunday night again."

He nods. "I had Saturday and Sunday off. I went camping and fishing with a friend of mine. I gave you his name and number. Did you call him?"

"We did. Sunday night?" I remind him.

"He drove and dropped me off Sunday night around nine at my place. I hadn't had a shower all weekend and needed one. I put all my gear in the garage. The car was there when I did. I went up to my apartment and took a very long shower. Then I grabbed a beer and kicked back on the couch until I fell asleep. When I woke up the next morning I was still on the couch. I got up and around, went downstairs, and that's when I realized the car was gone. Mr. Aaron was still sleeping. I don't know. I guess I figured the housekeeper borrowed it. Sometimes she does that if her car is giving her problems. Mr. Aaron doesn't mind. Honestly, I didn't think anything about it. There's a car seat in the truck as well, so I used that one for the day."

It's exactly what he said before, verbatim. Normally, when you ask someone to recount, it's not word for exact word.

"Did you see Scarlett in the car when you put your gear in the garage?" I ask.

"No, I would have told you if I had."

"You didn't leave your apartment for anything? A smoke? A walk around the property? A quick run into town?"

He shakes his head.

"Did you teach Scarlett to drive that car?"

Gerald doesn't answer.

"Gerald?"

He sighs. "Yes. But you don't understand, her parents don't let her do anything. They treated her like she was five instead of thirteen. There was a reason why she didn't just go home that night. She took advantage of what little freedom she had. That's why she liked visiting me. We had fun, ya know?"

"Cool Uncle Gerald."

"Yeah, isn't that part of being an uncle? I get to break the rules a little?"

"What rules do you break?" I ask.

"Innocent stuff like letting her eat junk food for dinner. Watching movies her parents won't allow. She loved horror films, but her mom thought they were satanic. We only drove the car around the property and maybe down the road a bit. We didn't go far. I promise. Listen, there's stuff she wanted to do that I wouldn't allow."

"Like?"

"Well, a few weeks ago I caught her on my laptop chatting with someone. When I asked her who, she got flustered. Listen, I've seen enough of those true crime things to know how pedophiles prey on innocent kids. I got onto her about it, and she apologized, but still. Even cool Uncle Gerald has a line. I love my nieces very much."

"We're going to need that laptop," I say.

FORTY-SIX

Saturday, 1:15 p.m.

BACK AT THE STATION, Vaughn gives the laptop to our tech team. The video from the country store hit my inbox. Together we begin reviewing it.

The country store sits alongside the one road in and out of the spa. The only other things of note along the way are mountain homes. This makes reviewing the video fairly easy, as not much traffic comes and goes on a switchback road once it's dark out. Between the hours of eight and midnight, I count exactly seven vehicles, none a white Mercedes.

Unless Mrs. Alexander was in a different car... "'*It's not a car that exactly blends in. If I'm truly going to spy on him, I need a different vehicle.*' That's what she said." I look at Vaughn. "Let's watch it again."

He rewinds, this time freezing on each vehicle and zooming in on the drivers. At 9:05 a familiar maroon SUV goes past the country store coming down the mountain from the spa. I narrow in on the driver and Lyft sticker, before scrolling to the back seat. There's someone there, though in the darkness I can't make out who. Our tech team probably can, though.

I've got my eyes focused on the screen when my phone rings. I don't bother checking who it is. I simply answer, "Detective Brach here."

A beat of static ticks by.

I look at my screen. It's a Georgia number but I don't recognize it. "Hello?"

A deep voice comes through. "Nell? It's your father."

A chilly numbness settles over me. I was a teenager the last time I spoke to or saw my father. His voice sounds odd, yet familiar.

"Tyler gave me your number," he says.

Gradually, the chill in my body warms, but the numbness stays, going from shock to emotional distance. My words come robotically. "What do you want?"

"I've been talking and emailing with your brother."

I knew about the latter, but Tyler didn't tell me he'd been talking with our father as well. "And?"

"I'd like to see Tyler, and you, of course. Your mom too if she's up to it. But I didn't want to just show up. I know you're Tyler's legal guardian and the head of the family. I wanted to clear it with you first."

The numbness lifts. The warmth in my body heats, flushing up into my neck and face. Pushing away from my desk, I stand. "Who the hell do you think you are? Tyler was a toddler the last time I saw you. Do you think you can just stroll back into our lives? Do you have any idea what we've all been through? We're just now getting a bit of normalcy, and you, what, suddenly have an attack of conscience? No, no you cannot see me or Tyler." I don't give him a chance to respond. I hang up.

My hands are shaking. I fist them tight, pressing them to my forehead. I can't deal with another family crisis. I just got a handle on Tyler. What is he thinking about talking to our father? I know exactly what he's thinking. He doesn't remember all the shit he put Mom through—coming and going for periodic booty calls, never taking responsibility for his two children, no child support, hell, never even fully admitting we *were* his children—and now this?

"Nell?" Vaughn touches my shoulder. "Are you okay?"

"I'm fine," I snap. I print a screenshot of the maroon SUV with the Lyft sticker. "Let's go."

FORTY-SEVEN

Saturday, 2:05 *p.m.*

BACK AT THE Lyft driver's apartment, Charlotte Swift answers the door again. This time her face is washed clean. She looks between us, smiling broadly. "Hi, did you forget something?"

I'm in no mood for a happy person. I get right to the point, holding up the screenshot. "Is this you?"

"Yes."

"You didn't tell us that you work in the Gatlinburg area as well," I snap.

She blinks, startled at my abruptness. "Oh, I'm sorry. I-I didn't know I was supposed to."

Vaughn holds a hand up. "It's okay. Tell us who's in the back seat and where you took the person."

"Sure." Charlotte motions us into her apartment.

It's been a few hours since we were here. Between stacks of folded clean clothes, the smell of wood polish, and couch cushions back in place, she's made progress in her spring cleaning. "Let me just get my phone," she says, disappearing down the hall.

I'd like to see Tyler, and you, of course. My jaw clenches. I look at Vaughn. "You better handle the questions. She doesn't deserve the mood I'm in right now."

"Agreed," my partner says.

She comes back with her phone, once again bringing up the app. "Her name is Yvonne Hardy. I took her from some fancy spa in Gatlinburg to the rock quarry here in White Quail." She shows us her phone. "I made good time. Got her there at 9:31 p.m."

Yvonne Hardy, Mary-Anne Alexander's mother.

"Are you sure her name was Yvonne Hardy?" Vaughn asks.

"That's what it says right here." Charlotte points to her screen. "Wait a minute." She frowns as she pinches Yvonne's photo and zooms in. "That wasn't who I gave a ride to. The woman I gave a ride to was much younger and very plastic surgery if you know what I mean. Fake boobies and puffy lips."

Vaughn shows her a photo of Mary-Anne Alexander.

"Yes!" The driver enthusiastically nods. "That's her."

"When you got to the rock quarry, did you see anybody there? Or any other vehicles?" I ask though I told Vaughn to do the questions.

"Yeah, a guy was waiting. The girl even made a joke about how if he wasn't so great in bed, she wouldn't bother with these weird booty call locations. I felt super awkward. I let her out and drove away."

"What did the guy look like?"

"Blond, fit, average height, and probably early thirties."

"And the car?"

"It wasn't dark, like black or blue. It was light, but not white. Maybe crème or tan?" Charlotte shrugs.

Vaughn says, "If I were to show you four different vehicles, could you identify which one it is?"

"Probably."

On his phone, he finds four random photos of cars in variations of light colors. Three are incorrect and one is spot on.

Charlotte flips through them, instantly identifying the right one—the tan Nissan. "What's going on?" she asks.

"Do you not watch the news?" I bite off.

She falls silent. An awkward few seconds tick by. Quietly she says, "No, I don't. It depresses me."

"You should reconsider. That young girl you gave a ride to? She's dead. That tan Nissan? She was in it. You were one of the last people to see her alive. We could have used your information on this a hell of a lot earlier."

My response is harsh, unfair, and misdirected. It's not my proudest moment. I'm fully aware my unprofessionalism has everything to do with my father.

FORTY-EIGHT

The night it happened

SCARLETT WISHED her best friend wouldn't have gone with Bennett. He wanted to "party," which meant alcohol, smoking, and whatever else. Partying just wasn't something Scarlett wanted to do. Elle did, though. Lately, she'd been acting so different. They used to like the same stuff—movies, old board games, and crafts—but now Elle seemed so focused on boys and being popular.

Uncle Gerald said that sometimes friends grow up and apart. Scarlett hoped that wasn't happening. Though it was partly her fault too. There was stuff she did that she kept secret from her best friend. Mostly because Elle had a big mouth, and Scarlett didn't want everyone to know her business.

Like how she snuck out of the courthouse every Friday and went to Depot Hill. At first, she went just to see. Her parents warned her that Depot Hill was the "bad" part of town. But it wasn't bad at all. She loved it there, and she started to make friends. Like Mr. Alexander. Sure, he was old enough to be her grandfather, but she liked him. He listened to her when she spoke. He asked questions. He cared. He wanted her to have a life she never thought possible. He wanted her to see the world. And she wanted that, so very badly. She just didn't know how to tell her parents. Her mom had said more than once how much she couldn't wait for Scarlett to go on her first date to the end-of-year school dance. Her mom had already suggested a few boys that Scarlett could go with.

But Scarlett didn't like boys. She liked girls.

Or rather one girl in particular. Her name was Xia. First, what an awesome name. But mostly, she understood Scarlett. They "clicked" as Uncle Gerald would've said. They met at the hospital where they both volunteered. She was one year older than Scarlett and attended an online high school. Xia lived in the neighborhood by the rock quarry. Scarlett had never been to the quarry. Xia loved going there at night to look at the stars. She'd described them in such great detail that Scarlett had begun sketching her words. One day Scarlett would join her, and they'd look at the stars together.

They also talked secretly online.

Uncle Gerald caught them once and thought Scarlett was messaging a creepy old man pretending to be younger. He gave her a big talk that she patiently listened to. She loved her uncle. She didn't think he'd mind that she liked Xia, but she wasn't ready to tell him yet.

When the Lyft driver dropped her off at her uncle's place, Scarlett planned on waiting for him to get home. She'd had a headache for the past couple of hours and needed some Tylenol. Uncle Gerald would have some. She got into his car, and in the dark, she quietly stared through the windshield and up at the stars.

Was Xia looking at the same stars?

A few more minutes went by. Scarlett squeezed her eyes shut. She pressed her fingers into the sides of her head. She'd been getting a lot of headaches recently. Uncle Gerald also got them. He thought she might need glasses. She opened the glove compartment, rifling through. She found napkins, a protein bar, paperwork for the car, a pack of gum, and finally her uncle's bottle of Tylenol. She shook out two green pills and put the bottle back. She thought Tylenol was white, but she could be wrong. This was probably a different strength or something. She carried water in her book bag and drank several gulps to get the pills down, then she climbed into the back.

A child's seat took up one part with a large rolled-up blanket beside it. Using her book bag as a pillow, Scarlett stretched out the length of the floorboard and covered herself with the blanket. She closed her eyes and willed her headache to go away.

Time flowed by. Her body began to drift with her thoughts. She felt light and free like she could spread her arms and fly. She couldn't ever remember feeling this way before.

She slept. She dreamed of stars.

A faint sound entered her dreams—an engine and doors opening and closing. Her uncle's voice echoed. "Thanks for the lift home and a great weekend."

Hi, Uncle Gerald. She smiled.

The engine faded into the sound of water running above her. It reminded her of the sound at her house when she took a shower.

She sank further into sleep. She dreamed of holding hands with Xia. She dreamed of kissing Xia.

The door to her uncle's car opened. She smiled again. *Where are we going, Uncle Gerald? Do I get to drive?*

He started the car. He drove away.

The movement rocked her, sending her sliding further into oblivion. Her head didn't hurt anymore. That was nice.

Uncle Gerald rolled down the windows. He turned on the radio. "Sweet Home Alabama" floated from the speakers. He sang along to the lyrics. She liked his voice. She tried to sing with him, but she couldn't get her throat to make a noise.

Maybe because this was a dream. If it were real life, she'd be up front next to her uncle singing with him. She'd have to remember to tell him that she dreamt of him. He'd like this story.

A chilly breeze flowed across her. She snuggled further under the blanket. Darkness moved across her brain. She saw nothing. She heard nothing.

Then a woman spoke, her voice outside the car. "Hi."

"Hi, back," Uncle Gerald said, his voice outside the car too. "In the mood for a little...green fun?" he asked.

"Oh, yeah. Let's split one though. We both got way too loopy last time."

"No, we both passed out last time."

She laughed. "My point."

"Next time we'll try ecstasy."

"I'm down with that."

Pills rattled around in a bottle. Scarlett thought they sounded funny, especially when the pills took form, holding hands and dancing with tutus. She'd never had such a weird dream. She'd have to remember to tell Xia about the dancing green pills. Xia would love that.

She wasn't sure how much time went by, but the green pills kept dancing and dancing.

The car dipped like someone climbed onto the hood. Her uncle and the woman both giggled. Scarlett tried to giggle with them, but again she couldn't make the sound come from her mouth.

The car moved—back and forth, back and forth—swaying her. She liked being cocooned under the blanket. She liked being rocked to sleep.

She heard noises that embarrassed her. She'd once heard her parents make those noises.

The car slid. Her uncle and the woman gasped. Then, they laughed.

"Just leave it," the woman said, laughing, laughing, laughing. "Let's go!"

The sound of running footsteps receded as Scarlett sank peacefully, and once again, into slumber.

Sink, sank, sunk.

Whichever tense, she loved the feeling.

Down.

Down.

Down.

Slowly, water coated her body. She didn't mind. She loved the water. She loved swimming.

Her brain fogged. Her thoughts halted.

She inhaled. Why did it hurt to breathe?

Her eyes fought to stay closed, but she pried them open. She saw a dark blur. This wasn't a dream. This was a nightmare. She needed to wake up. Now. Now! NOW.

Her mouth opened. Water gushed in. She screamed. And gagged. And screamed.

The fuzziness that had distorted her thoughts, lifted. She thrashed. She kicked. She punched. She batted at the blanket holding her down. She clawed at the handle of the back door.

It wouldn't open.

More water rushed in. The car sank further. She fought to leave. She fought for air. But something kept her in place. She kicked at it. Her shoe came off. Her chest squeezed. Her fingers gripped the window. She pulled herself through, ignoring the glass biting into her ribs. Her body lifted. She swam, hard.

Her mouth met air. She gulped it in, taking in more water. She fought her way to shore. Her hands and knees met rock. She pulled herself up. She ran from the water and into the woods. She didn't know where she was going. She simply needed to run.

Gasping, Scarlett tore through the dark woods. The tree limbs reached for her, like long scabby fingers, scraping at her clothes and skin. She slid across a patch of leaves and fallen pine needles, landing behind a cluster of shrubs. Her heart pounded, achingly fast. Her gaze darted through the night. The air around her pulsed with her nerves.

A cool April breeze curled through, and despite the adrenaline spiking in her veins, she shivered. Overhead, the moon glowed full. The pungent, yet sweet scent of the town's brewery clung in the air.

Across the woods, just over there, a welcoming yellow light outlined a home. She was just about to crawl forward when her lungs contracted.

She coughed.

She tried to yell for help, but no words came.

Only...silence.

FORTY-NINE

Saturday, 3:45 p.m.

WHEN WE ARRIVE at Jack and Gerald's childhood home, several vehicles are now parked in the driveway. The garage door is up with Gerald standing just inside, smoking a cigarette and staring out at us as we park.

I don't know where to start with this man. I don't have to. He sees his guilt all over my face as I walk toward him.

Tears flood his eyes. "We didn't know she was in the car."

"She was scared, alone, drowning." Anger quivers through my voice. "She was thirteen goddamn years old. She had her whole life ahead of her. And for what? A booty call with Mary-Anne Alexander? Where's the Rohypnol?"

"I threw it away."

"How did your niece get it?"

"I keep it in a small Tylenol bottle in my glove box. I never give it to women without consent. I promise. I always take it with them. It's a party drug."

"A party drug your niece accidentally took."

"She got headaches," he whispers.

The garage door that leads into the house opens. Jack and Nina appear. "What's going on?" Jack asks.

"Oh God." With the cigarette still between his fingers, Gerald covers his face with his hands. "What have I done?"

Jack takes a step forward. Vaughn shifts toward him.

Crying, Gerald turns toward his brother. "We didn't know, Jack. I swear."

"Know what?" Jack looks at me.

The cigarette tumbles from Gerald's fingers. He staggers. "If I had known—" his breath catches— "I would've gone in after her. You've got to believe me."

Jack falls mute.

Nina gasps.

"Don't be mad," Gerald sobs. "Please don't be mad at me." He reaches out a hand. His face crumbles. "I'm sorry."

Nina screams. She flies across the garage and smacks him. She kicks him. She hits him. Jack does nothing but numbly stare.

Grasping Nina, I pull her off Gerald. She collapses against me, weeping.

He falls to his knees, pleading. "I'm sorry. I didn't know. I didn't know," he wails.

Vaughn pulls out cuffs.

"Gerald Macadem, you are under arrest for the murder of Scarlett Macadem."

FIFTY

One month later

GERALD MACADEM and Mary-Anne Alexander were charged with manslaughter. Despite Ian Alexander's enormous bank account and round-the-clock legal advice, he's offered no support for his wife. He filed for divorce within twenty-four hours of her being arrested. According to the prenup, he walks away free and clear due to her felony arrest and infidelity.

His son is another matter.

Bennett Alexander has been identified as the person behind reinventing The Quiet Game. Evidence led to charges of harassment and unlawful sexual activity for not only Bennett but several others as well. He was expelled from school and is awaiting trial.

The game has officially been put to rest.

"Nell, Vaughn." The sheriff looks between us. "Fabulous work with everything. If two people ever deserved a long weekend, it's you two. I don't want to see you back here until Monday morning."

"You don't have to tell me twice." Vaughn logs out of his laptop and stands.

"Hey, how'd it go in Nashville?" He decided to speak at the parole hearing after all.

"Denied for another year."

"I'm glad, Vaughn."

A slight smile curves his face. "Thanks." He grabs his sunglasses off his desk. "See you Monday."

After closing down my station, I send a quick text to Tyler.

Me: Don't forget you have an algebra quiz due by 4 pm.
Tyler: Already did it! Made an A :)
Me: That's great!

Tyler is thriving in his new online school. It's private and costs more money than is in my budget, but I'm making it work. He loves it, and that is all that matters.

I walk outside the station to see Ronan Aaron stepping from his sports car. We've barely spoken in the past month. What words we have shared have been polite hellos and goodbyes.

It's time for more.

"Hey." I walk toward him across the lot.

He comes up short, surprised to see me, sure, but more that I just spoke to him. "Hello."

"Didn't expect to see you here."

He points to the bloodmobile parked in front of the station. "I'm donating."

"Oh." Suddenly nervous, I shift my weight and tuck my

hands into my windbreaker. "Um, listen, the past month has been insane. Now that Scarlett's case has wrapped, I wanted to..."

What did I want? To pick up where we left off? To start over? To mend faces? To speak again? To be friends?

Ronan closes the distance between us, not touching me but pretty damn close. Oddly, I don't feel the usual anticipatory flutters. I feel more resigned. Like I'm just now realizing whatever we had is over.

And I'm okay with that.

His voice comes quiet, intimate. "Nell, I was profoundly sad after my wife died. You were the first woman to draw my interest. We met each other at the right time. We needed each other and the distraction it offered. You are a beautiful, strong, capable, intelligent woman. I'm honored you spent time with me. But it's okay. We both know this is over."

"You just read my thoughts."

We share a smile.

"Friends?" he says.

"Definitely." I step away. "Next time I'm at the courthouse I'll come to say hi."

"I'd like that very much."

He stays right there, watching me walk to my vehicle, climb in, and drive off. It's only after I turn the corner and look into the rearview that he finally goes into the bloodmobile.

Yeah, I'm okay with that. He's right, we met at a time when we both needed the distraction. It's time for us to move on.

Sometime later, I pull into my neighborhood and our home. A black Toyota Camry sits parked where Grandpa's truck used to be. Mom drives it now to her new job at Starbucks. She's still living with Olivia, and though I won't say Mom and Tyler are doing great, they at least talk now.

I note the Georgia tags right as the front door to our house opens. Tyler emerges. He looks panicked. "What are you doing home?"

"Sheriff Owens gave me the afternoon off." My eyes narrow. "Why? Whose car is that?"

Tyler cringes. "Don't be angry."

A man appears behind him, tall with thinning brown hair. "Hello, Nell."

"Dad."

OTHER BOOKS BY S. E. GREEN

The Lady Next Door

The Family

Sister Sister

The Strangler

The Suicide Killer

Monster

The Third Son

Vanquished

Mother May I

Ultimate Sacrifice

Unseen

S. E. Green is the award-winning, best-selling author of young adult and adult fiction. She grew up in Tennessee where she dreaded all things reading and writing. She didn't read her first book for enjoyment until she was twenty-five. After that, she was hooked! When she's not writing, she loves traveling and hanging out with a rogue armadillo that frequents her coastal Florida home.